*"I hope I live up to your expectations, Gavin."*

Gavin's expression softened at Meg's words, and he squeezed her hand gently. "Don't worry. All these years of training horses has made me a pretty good judge of character. I know you're going to be good for my son."

"Does that mean horses are a lot like people, or that I'm a lot like a horse?" she asked with a crooked grin.

He chuckled and rocked back on his heels. "As a matter of fact, your legs are as well shaped as any filly's I've ever seen."

Then Gavin gently tilted her face up to his. "I like you, Meg. You have very expressive eyes. They tell what's in your heart."

If that was true, Meg was in big trouble because right now, she was feeling quite smitten with the man before her. And that wasn't what she wanted to feel for a man she'd just met.

Dear Reader,

June is traditionally the month of weddings, and at Silhouette Romance, wedding bells are definitely ringing! Our heroines this month will fulfill their hearts' desires with the kinds of heroes you've always dreamed of—from the dark, mysterious stranger to the lovable boy-next-door. Silhouette Romance novels *always* reflect the magic of love—sweeping you away with heartwarming, poignant stories that will move you time and time again.

In the next few months, we'll be publishing romances by many of your all-time favorites, including Diana Palmer, Brittany Young and Annette Broadrick. And, as promised, Nora Roberts begins her CALHOUN WOMEN series this month with the Silhouette Romance, *Courting Catherine.*

WRITTEN IN THE STARS is a very special event for 1991. Each month, we're proud to present a Silhouette Romance that focuses on the hero—and his astrological sign. June features one of the most enigmatic, challenging men of all—*The Gemini Man.* Our authors and editors have created this delightfully romantic series especially for you, the reader, and we'd love to hear what you think. After all, at Silhouette Romance, we take our readers' comments to heart!

Please write to us at Silhouette Romance
300 East 42nd Street
New York, NY 10017

We look forward to hearing from you!

Sincerely,

Valerie Susan Hayward
Senior Editor

# DARLENE PATTEN

# A Place Called Home

*Silhouette* *Romance*

Published by Silhouette Books New York

**America's Publisher of Contemporary Romance**

For Chicago-North RWA—
Thanks for your support and wonderful critiques.
And for Jimmie Morel—
An especial thank you for a special friend.

SILHOUETTE BOOKS
300 E. 42nd St., New York, N.Y. 10017

A PLACE CALLED HOME

ISBN: 0-373-08800-0

First Silhouette Books printing June 1991

Printed in the U.S.A.

**Books by Darlene Patten**

Silhouette Romance

*A Half-Dozen Reasons* #570
*A Place Called Home* #800

---

## *DARLENE PATTEN*

met her husband in ballroom-dancing class during college, and they made great partners on more than just the dance floor. What could be a more perfect match than a landscape architect and an interior designer? He designed the outside of their home, she designed the inside, and together they designed three sons who fill their lives with activity and joy. Writing romances is a natural occupation for Darlene, who considers her life one long "happily ever after."

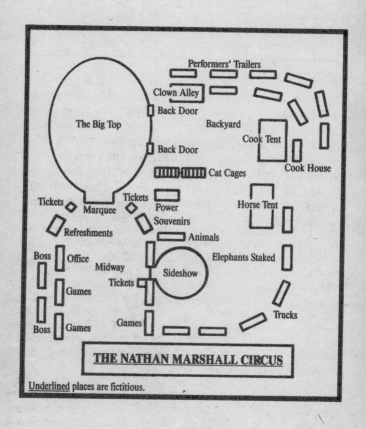

Performers' Trailers

Clown Alley

Back Door

The Big Top

Backyard

Cook Tent

Back Door

Cook House

Cat Cages

Tickets

Tickets

Power

Horse Tent

Marquee

Souvenirs

Refreshments

Animals

Boss    Office

Elephants Staked

Midway

Sideshow

Tickets

Games

Boss    Games

Games

Trucks

## THE NATHAN MARSHALL CIRCUS

Underlined places are fictitious.

# *Chapter One*

"**D**on't look now, but you're being followed again."

Her friend's quiet comment made Meg Harper stop and turn in the middle of the midway where they'd just purchased snow cones at the gaily painted concession stand.

"Really? Where is he?" Perusing the row of game booths for the child who'd been shadowing her all morning, Meg nibbled at the syrupy slush, anxious for the comfort of the cool raspberry-flavored liquid on her parched throat. Since arriving yesterday on the grounds of the traveling circus, now located in Illinois, the combination of unseasonably dry wind, swirling dust and ninety-degree temperatures had made her feel as if she was slowly being desiccated. Snow cones had come to be her salvation.

"He's over by the sideshow tent," Carol told her, slipping her free arm through Meg's and dragging her in the opposite direction. "Come on. You don't want to encourage him. You spend enough time with kids his age the rest of the year."

"But he looks lonely," Meg protested, her heart going out to the little boy with the soulful brown eyes who was peeping at them from around the corner of one of the semitrailers that formed the entrance to the sideshow. If it weren't for his cowboy boots, the child could have passed for a young Huck Finn. His straight brown hair stuck out helter-skelter as if he didn't know combs existed, and his bare chest was tanned to a light nut brown beneath his dusty denim overalls.

"Listen, Meg, in ten weeks our summer job with the circus will be over, and we'll be back to teaching kids like him. For now we need to take advantage of our freedom and mix with other adults, preferably of the male variety, if you catch my drift. It's time for us to live it up a little." Carol hugged herself. "Ooh, I get goose bumps just thinking about the traveling we get to do this summer."

Meg knew her friend was speaking figuratively since it was a physical impossibility to work up a set of goose bumps on such a hot day, but she couldn't help smiling at Carol's enthusiasm. Unfortunately for Meg, all the moving around she'd done as a child made the thought of travel less than appealing. In fact, if it hadn't been for Carol's pleading, Meg wouldn't have joined this circus at all. In Meg's opinion, performing their clown act for kids' parties and other functions back home in Rockford would have been preferable to traipsing all over the country in a camper. But knowing that Carol had never had the opportunity to travel any farther than Chicago, she'd agreed to her friend's request.

"It should be interesting," Meg said, unwilling to rain on Carol's parade, even though she doubted her friend would be seeing the traveling circus through such rose-tinted glasses by the end of the summer. After all, one shopping center was pretty much like another. Meg doubted that Carol had investigated the circus route before joining up, though.

"Hey, look at that!" Carol pointed to an elephant being washed by a scruffy-looking keeper.

Meg stopped beside her friend and watched with interest. They were taking this early-afternoon walk to acquaint themselves with the layout of the circus since there hadn't

een time after they had arrived yesterday. It had been too
lose to show time so they'd merely sat in on that evening's
wo performances to familiarize themselves with the clown
outines they would be taking part in the next day, then gone
o bed after the last show. Rising early, they'd rehearsed
vith Clancy, the head clown, and met with the bandmaster
o discuss the music for one of their own acts. Now, with a
ew hours to themselves before performing in their first
how, they were anxious to look around the place they
vould be calling home for the next ten weeks.

Glancing over her shoulder, Meg noticed that she was still
eing tailed by the little boy. Seeing that she'd spotted him,
e quickly ducked behind two men who were practicing their
uggling. Meg smiled, wondering what kind of game the
oungster was up to.

A blast of cold water in the chest made her jump in sur-
rise. "Aack!" Her attention flew back to the elephants.

"Sorry, ma'am," the keeper apologized as he tried to grab
he hose back from a recalcitrant elephant. The large beast
wung the hose back and forth with his trunk, making the
vater arc and splash on whatever, or whomever, was un-
ucky enough to be in the way. Carol, who'd obviously seen
t coming, had jumped back in time.

Meg laughed, tugging her sodden yellow T-shirt away
rom her chest. "No problem," she called back, relieved
hat she had on a bra beneath the clinging fabric. "Now that
'm over the shock, the soaking feels pretty good. He prob-
bly did me a favor."

"*She,*" the man stressed. "This here's Mabel. All our
ulls are female."

"Female bulls?" Carol questioned. "Isn't that a contra-
liction in terms?"

"Show talk, ma'am. We call all the elephants bulls. Might
ay it's 'cause they're so bullheaded."

"Well, tell Mabel thanks," Meg replied. "A shower was
ust what I needed."

The man nodded his head and smiled, revealing a crooked row of tobacco-stained teeth, then grabbed the hose and rinsed the soap from the elephant's back.

Strolling on, the two women passed five good-looking muscular men headed toward the big top. Meg recognized them as the Alexander Brothers, who did balancing and teeterboard acts. Noticing her friend's expression—Carol was practically drooling—Meg couldn't help but issue a warning.

"Carol, unless you plan to give up your teaching job and live the gypsy life from now on, I suggest that you don't fall for any of the men around here. This may be a working vacation for us, but for most of these people the circus is the way they make their living."

"I suppose you're right," Carol agreed and sighed wistfully. "But there are an awful lot of hunks in this circus who will be hard to resist."

The women stepped underneath the large awning of the horse tent and Meg plopped down on a bale of hay, leaning back against another in the large stack as she sucked the sweet nectar from the ice in her snow cone. "Don't get too tragic. You can still date them. If I know you, you'll have men lined up outside our camper all summer waiting for your attention."

"You sound like I'm the only one," Carol protested. "What about you?"

Meg waved her hand dismissively. "You know I'm more the Pied Piper type. Attracting males like my little shadow is more my style. I think we lost him, by the way," she said, peering around.

"Oh, you're hopeless!" Carol scowled and shook her fist in mock anger. "You make me crazy. If you'd flirt a little you'd have no problem attracting men."

"Well, then I guess I'll just have to stay single," Meg said stubbornly. "I hate playing coy games." Besides which, she wasn't any good at it and she knew it. There was nothing enjoyable about getting flustered, embarrassed and tonguetied, which she always seemed to do when a man approached her.

Carol's deep sigh made Meg smile. It was apparent that her friend considered her a lost cause.

"I'm going over to the big top and watch those guys work out. Do you want to come?" Carol asked.

Meg shook her head. "No, I think I'm just going to sit here and conserve my energy for the shows tonight."

She watched her friend stride off, then turned to gaze at the long row of tethered horses. They were beautiful animals, but looked as listless as she felt. "Heat's got you guys down, too, eh?"

"Yep. Hell of a day, isn't it?" The deep male voice came from the hay behind her and she jumped up and turned in shock.

"Who said that?"

A man's head slowly rose over the stack of hay, followed by a pair of muscular shoulders clad in a white T-shirt. He moved forward, resting his tanned forearms on the top bale as he knelt on the other side, and his brown eyes twinkled with amusement. "I did."

Meg gulped as she was momentarily caught off guard by his sexy grin. His slightly long and carelessly styled brown hair gave him a rough-edged look, but it was the knowing glint in his eyes that had such a breathtaking effect on her.

Exasperated by her reaction to him, she scowled. "What's the big idea of scaring me half to death?"

He shrugged, unrepentant. "I figure you deserved it after waking me up."

"Oh." No doubt that accounted for the piece of hay stuck to his shoulder that her fingers itched to brush away. "Sorry."

"That's all right. I found your conversation *very* interesting."

"You eavesdropped?" Meg felt her eyes grow large as she recalled her discussion with Carol.

He placed a hand over his heart. "Forgive me, but I was so shocked by what I heard that I just couldn't interrupt. Do you really hate to flirt?"

Mortified, Meg felt the heat spread through her body and up into her face. Embarrassment always put her on the defensive. She raised her chin. "So what if I do? I don't think that it's any of your concern."

"Uh-oh. Don't get mad. I think it's great to meet a woman who doesn't feel it's necessary to play games."

"Oh, really?" she asked, trying to decide if he was being sincere.

He nodded. "Your approach is much more direct."

"My approach?"

"Sure. A wet T-shirt will catch a man's eye every time. You look very attractive in yours, by the way."

Meg inhaled sharply, shocked at his boldness. Seeing the devilish glitter in his eyes, she knew he was immensely enjoying baiting her. How she longed to make a clever retort that would put him in his place, but verbal sparring with men had never been her forte. She was sure Carol would have been able to make some kind of witty rejoinder to turn the situation to her advantage, but for the life of her, Meg couldn't think of a single thing to say. All she knew was that she suddenly felt very uncomfortable in her damp T-shirt and had to change. Turning on her heel, she marched off toward the trailer with the sound of his laughter ringing in her ears.

"You blew it, Dad." His son's brown eyes held a glimmer of disgust and small shoulders drooped in disappointment as the boy threw himself down next to his father in the hay.

"Huh? What did I do now, Dennis?" Gavin Warner asked, automatically reaching out to smooth the hair his son was always in too much of a hurry to comb.

"That was *her*, Dad."

"Her?"

"The teacher."

"The teacher? Oh . . . Ooh." Gavin sucked in his breath as he realized to whom his son was referring. He quickly looked over his shoulder at the stiff-backed woman in yellow who was striding away from him. Knowing he was the one to have angered her gave him a sick feeling in the pit of his stomach. His son was right. He'd blown it.

Dennis nodded his head. "Boy, I followed her all morning so I could talk to her alone. But I didn't get to. How come you teased her like that, anyway?"

Gavin squirmed under his son's critical stare and wondered how a look from a six-year-old could make him feel remorse for his contrary ways when no amount of punishment from an adult had ever had such a strong effect. "I'm sorry, son. I wish I hadn't, believe me." Irritated with himself, Gavin ran his hand through his hair and sighed, contemplating how to go about explaining his actions.

"It's like this, Dennis," he said slowly. "When a man feels attracted to a woman, he sometimes gives her a difficult time. That's his way of defending himself against the feelings he's not sure he wants to feel. Do you understand?"

Gavin watched his son mull it over. It would be a miracle if Dennis caught what he was trying to get across. He wasn't sure *he* even understood what he'd said.

"I think I do," the boy replied, his brow furrowed in concentration. "Is it kind of like when the lions wrestle around together before they mate?"

Gavin felt his stomach drop to his boots. He knew his mouth had dropped wide open as well, but couldn't seem to help it. What the hell kind of reply was he supposed to make to that? Forcing his jaws closed through sheer willpower, he cleared his throat, wishing there was a more experienced parent nearby whom he could quickly consult. Not really happy with the comparison, he could see the boy's point and managed to choke out, "I guess you might put it that way, Dennis, but please don't repeat what you just said to anyone. They might not understand."

"Okay." The boy shrugged his shoulders in an attitude that displayed that he couldn't care less. "But what are we going to do about the teacher, Dad? She might not want to help me now that you made her mad."

"Well, how about the other one?" Gavin asked hopefully. "Her friend's a teacher, too, isn't she?"

Dennis's sigh conveyed what he thought of the question, and Gavin knew he'd blundered again.

"Oh, Dad. I told you before. *She* teaches art. Miss Harper's the one who teaches the reg'lar stuff."

"Oh, yes, of course. Now I remember," he was quick to reply, though in actuality he didn't remember the specifics at all. Between his work schedule and Dennis's bout of stomach flu, Gavin had been awake for thirty hours straight and he'd been anxious to finish feeding the horses that morning. He hadn't paid very close attention to his son's ramblings about the teacher who'd joined the circus. All he remembered was giving his son permission to ask the teacher if she'd be willing to teach him to read. Other than that, Gavin's mind had been on going to bed. After completing his chores, he'd stretched out on the hay for some long-awaited sleep, too tired to drag himself back to his trailer.

"Don't worry, son. I'll give her a chance to cool off, and then I'll go apologize to Miss Harper and get this matter straightened out." *Miss Harper.* He had trouble connecting the name with the woman. In Gavin's mind, the name implied a gray-haired little old lady with bifocals perched on the end of her nose, not the long-legged beauty with thick, wavy chestnut-colored tresses. But knowing how anxious his son was to learn to read, Gavin didn't care what she looked like.

Now that Dennis was old enough to start first grade in the fall, Gavin knew he had some decisions to make. Should he sign Dennis up for correspondence courses as the other circus children had been, or should he settle down someplace so Dennis could go to school? As a boy, Gavin had been dragged around the country and had changed schools as often as his mother had changed jobs. He didn't want that life for Dennis. He wanted something better for his son. He wanted Dennis to get a jump on learning to read.

Gavin ran his hand through his hair and sighed. Somehow he had to talk Miss Harper into teaching his son.

Dressed in full clown costume from the top of her redwigged head down to her oversize floppy shoes, Meg stood with Carol and the rest of the clown troupe outside the performers' entrance to the big top and anxiously waited for the first parade to begin. Her mind savored the moment, committing it to memory. This was the circus, the big time, an experience a long way from their school's Spring Talent Show where she and Carol had performed their first clown act over six years before.

Though Meg hadn't been enthusiastic about traveling, she couldn't help but get excited over the prospect of performing before a huge tent full of people. She was a little nervous, but knew her stage fright would take care of itself once she got in front of the crowd. She was able to do things as bossy, brazen Big Bertha, her clown character, that she'd never dream of doing as herself. Being quiet and conservative, she admired people who were slightly flamboyant, so had styled her clown character after that type of person.

On the other hand, Carol, who was normally outgoing, had created a sweet, demure character she called Pansy. Together, the two clown personalities complemented each other—as did the personalities of the two people who portrayed them. Meg and Carol had turned their hobby into second careers, performing at charity benefits, parties, and in parades, until Carol had latched on to the idea of joining the traveling circus for the summer.

Now, third in line behind the flag-bearing mounted horses and the band, Meg looked around at the rest of the performers and could feel the tension in the air heighten as everyone mentally prepared for the curtain to open. She had never felt quite so keyed up before a performance. Her anticipation had to be due to this being the circus. There was, after all, a higher expectation on the part of the audience because they were attending a circus, but that wasn't all. There was something magical about the circus, and Meg couldn't help feeling a little special because she was part of it.

Hearing the first few notes of music, she felt her heart hammer so hard she had to breathe deeply to keep from suffocating. When the band began to move forward, excitement fizzed inside her like a bottle of soda that had been shaken.

"Here goes nothin'," Carol stated with a grin. "You're not nervous, are you?"

"Not too much," Meg answered. "It's the suspense that's killing me. Let's go!"

With the other clowns, she smiled and waved to the people in the crowded stands. The cacophony of sound around her, the bouncy band music, crashing symbols, the hoots, hollers, whistles, clapping, laughter and shouts, all combined into a deafening, blood-stirring roar as she made her way around the hippodrome track blowing huge bubbles from the wand of her giant-size bottle of suds. Knowing that she was actually a part of this grandest of the grand celebrations known as the circus made her glad she had agreed to come.

Meg observed the audience with fascination. Some youngsters were openmouthed with wonder at the big, wobbly bubbles that floated on the upward draft; others grinned in fiendish delight as they poked a finger at and burst as many bubbles as they could reach. Meg watched their expressions with satisfaction, thrilled each time a parent shared a smile with a child or lifted a wide-eyed toddler and pointed out something special. Every one of the thousand people in the big top that night would take home a happy memory, but Meg doubted if anyone would cherish it more than she.

As Meg exited through the performers' door into the area known as the backyard, where the show people lined up for their entrances, Nathan Marshall, the rotund ringmaster, was just introducing the first act.

"Ladieees and gentlemeeen, boys and girls, hold on to your hats and rope in your loved ones. Here comes the rootin'est, tootin'est Wild West Show east of the Mississippi. Say howdy to Pistol Pete McGrath and the Cowboy Revue!"

Meg, who had lingered a little longer than the rest of the clowns during the Spectacle Parade, had to jump back to avoid being run over by the stream of hooting, hollering cowboys on horseback galloping into the tent. She watched in amazement and actually felt the ground shake as they roared past. Looking up, she saw the little boy who'd been shadowing her all day bringing up the rear on a brown pony. Dressed in a matching outfit, the rider on the chestnut mare at his side was obviously his father, but Meg was shocked to see that the man was also the one with whom she'd had the humiliating encounter earlier that day.

She frowned as she watched them ride into the center ring and begin to perform rope tricks. The man she'd seen in the horse tent earlier had looked at her in a way no married man had a right to look. Though her experience with men was limited, she'd have had to be stupid not to realize he'd been coming on to her. Obviously he fancied himself as some sort of Don Juan. Meg decided it would be better to avoid him in the future.

Rushing to clown alley, she arrived just in time for a quick review of what she and Carol were expected to do during the next act. As she donned a black fireman's coat, boots and hat, all thoughts of the father and son were temporarily pushed to the back of her mind while she concentrated on her new role.

It wasn't until after the first show was over that Meg thought of them again. Sipping cold lemonade through a straw so she wouldn't mess up her makeup, she shifted in her wooden folding chair in clown alley and tried to get comfortable while waiting for the second show to begin. Several small groups of men and women sat around in shorts trying to keep cool, though they still had on their full makeup.

Meg, who'd removed her wig, put down her hairbrush and tugged at the fringe on her cutoffs. "Carol, did you see that little boy who's been following me around today in the Wild West act?"

Her friend looked up from the fingernail she'd been filing, but her eyes focused on a point above Meg's head and widened. Thinking the action rather curious, Meg was about to ask what was so interesting when she felt a hand on her shoulder. A man's low voice spoke into her ear. "Can I talk to you outside?"

Startled, Meg turned to look over her shoulder. It was *him*. She jumped up and faced the very man she'd planned to avoid. He was dressed in his fringed blue-and-white western-style shirt and pants and held a white Stetson in his hand.

"Do you always have to sneak up on people?" she demanded, irritated by the way her pulse had accelerated upon seeing him.

He smiled. "Sorry. I didn't mean to frighten you. Would you mind coming for a walk with me? There's something I'd like to discuss with you."

"I really don't think I'd be interested in anything you have to say," Meg stated, the memory of the difficult time he'd given her fresh in her mind. She heard Carol's gasp of surprise and was sure her friend thought she was making a big mistake, but Carol hadn't been embarrassed by him as Meg had been.

He grimaced and pulled on his ear, then looked at her contritely. "I deserve that, I know, but I came to apologize for the way I acted this afternoon, though I'd hoped to do it in private," he said quietly as his gaze shifted around the tent.

Meg became aware of several sets of eyes upon them and took a perverse pleasure in his discomfort. *Squirm,* she thought to herself.

He obviously read her mind, because he stared directly into her eyes and gave her a wry look. "You're enjoying this, aren't you?'' he mumbled just loud enough for her to hear.

Meg smiled in triumph.

"You win," he stated. With a sweeping flourish of his arm, he placed his Stetson over his heart and bowed, saying loudly, "Miss Harper, I apologize from the bottom of my heart. If you'd but grant the miserable wretch that I am your forgiveness, I'll be forever in your debt."

Snickers rose around them, and someone called out, "Gavin Warner, you been makin' a pest of yourself with that pretty gal already?"

Another male voice answered, "Hey, you know that Gavin don't let no grass grow under his feet when it comes to women."

Glad her white makeup covered her flaming cheeks, Meg said, "Perhaps we'd better continue our discussion somewhere else, Mr. Warner."

Gavin smiled. "An excellent idea, Miss Harper."

Hearing chuckles and wolf whistles following them out of the tent, Meg was scandalized to think that this man was pursuing her when he was married and had a son. Did he have no shame? Several steps outside the tent, Meg turned and faced him.

"What is it that you wanted, Mr. Warner?"

"Call me Gavin, Meg. The circus is like family. We don't stand on formalities." He slipped on the Stetson, tipping it down low on his forehead. "Let's get out of this sun. We can talk in my trailer."

"Is your wife there?"

"My wife?" His quick sideways glance held surprise. "Oh, you must mean because of Dennis. No, I'm divorced. Have been for four years." He nodded back toward clown alley and the look in his eyes told her he was aware of her suspicions regarding him. "Don't let what they just said in there fool you. With an active, curious son and a job that keeps me awake eighteen and sometimes twenty hours a day during the season, I don't have the time nor the energy to be a scoundrel. Satisfied?"

Meg nodded, ashamed of the way she'd misjudged him. "Now I owe you an apology," she admitted. "I'm afraid I jumped to the conclusion that you were sneaking around behind your wife's back. That wasn't very nice of me. I'm sorry."

He tsk-tsked, but smiled good-naturedly. "I guess I couldn't expect you to think anything different since you don't know me." His sideways glance sliced her way. "But that's a situation I'll remedy in the near future. If things work out the way I hope, we'll be seeing a lot of each other." He placed his hand on the small of her back as he guided her toward the group of performers' trailers.

## *Chapter Two*

Meg stepped inside Gavin's trailer, glad to be out of the blistering hot sun. Unfortunately it wasn't any cooler inside than it had been outside. Air-conditioning was obviously a luxury she wouldn't be seeing much of this summer.

Gavin gestured toward the seating area of the living room. "Make yourself comfortable."

"Thank you." She sat down on the brown corduroy sofa and pulled a tissue from her pocket. Carefully dabbing her sweaty brow, she tried not to mess up the clown makeup she'd painstakingly applied before the first show. As she glanced around, Meg took in the room's earth tones, sturdy furniture and animal artwork, but the most dominant feature that struck her about the all-male domain was its neatness. There wasn't a speck of clutter anywhere, no newspapers lying around, no toys underfoot, nothing out of place. She was impressed.

"Dennis," Gavin called. "Come meet Miss Harper."

Hearing the clap of footsteps on tile, Meg turned toward the kitchen doorway and saw her little shadow step into the room. She smiled at the milk mustache and cookie crumbs he wore in addition to the cowboy outfit she'd seen him in earlier.

"Hello, Dennis. It's nice to meet you at last."

Gavin pulled his son toward him and brushed off the boy's mouth, removing the remains of the child's snack, then nudged him forward.

Meg waited as Dennis approached her. Such a serious expression, she thought, wondering if he was nervous or merely trying to pick out her features through the clown makeup. Glancing at his father, she saw the apprehension duplicated. Something was up.

The boy extended his small hand, then quickly took it back and wiped it on his pants leg before shaking hers. "Hi."

Gavin strode to the brown-and-beige tweed chair across from Meg and sat slightly forward on its front edge. "Dennis has something he wants to ask you."

Meg raised her eyebrows. "Oh? Is that why you were following me around today?"

The child nodded, but didn't say anything, and glanced toward his father, as if for help.

Gavin pulled his son down to sit on one of his knees and absently rubbed the boy's back while he addressed Meg. "You noticed him, huh?" At her nod, he turned to Dennis. "Well, son, she's a teacher, all right. I've never met one yet who didn't have eyes in the back of her head."

Dennis grinned and murmured, "Daaad," then gave Meg a shy smile, rolling his eyes as if he was embarrassed by his father's comment.

Gavin shrugged with a smirk that said he couldn't help himself, and Meg laughed at his silliness. She realized, of course, that he'd tactfully eased his son's tension. Not all parents displayed such sensitivity toward their children's feelings. There was obviously more to this man than she'd originally thought.

"What did you want to ask me?" she questioned Dennis now that he seemed more at ease.

The boy studied the geometric pattern in the carpet, out-lining a diamond-shape with the toe of his boot.

"Well...since you're a teacher, I was wondering..." He peeked up through his long dark lashes. "I thought maybe you could teach me to read."

The request took Meg completely by surprise, but she tried not to show it.

Before she could reply, Gavin jumped in. "I'd pay you for lessons, of course. That is, if you're willing."

Meg couldn't refuse any child interested in learning to read and answered, "I'm willing, but doesn't the circus have a tutor?"

"No. The children get their lessons in the mail from a correspondence school," Gavin answered. "Dennis just turned six, so he'll be ready for first grade this fall. We hoped you'd be willing to give him a head start."

The father and son's anxiety as they awaited her answer was apparent. Meg realized that this was important to both of them. She had no desire to turn away a willing student. "I'll be happy to teach you, Dennis."

Gavin was the first to thank her. "You don't know how relieved I am to hear you say that. I'm glad what happened this afternoon didn't affect your decision."

Meg smiled at his rueful expression. "I'd never hold that against Dennis." She studied the child who was eyeing her bashfully. "Learning to read is important to you, isn't it, Dennis?"

The boy nodded. "Dad says that if I don't learn to read, I won't be able to be a vet when I grow up."

"A veterinarian?"

He nodded and his brown eyes sparkled with enthusi-asm.

Gavin squeezed the boy's shoulders. "Dennis will make a great doctor. He's always Johnny-on-the-spot when one of the animals gets sick or is injured, and it seems all he has to do is talk to them and they settle down." He grinned down at his son. "Nate Marshall nicknamed him Doctor Dolittle."

Meg was touched by the fatherly pride stamped on Gavin's features. He obviously had plans for his son's future. "Then I'll have to teach you to read for sure." She smiled at the boy. "We can't have you wasting your talent."

"What do you say, Dennis?" Gavin prompted.

"Thank you," the child replied automatically, sliding off his father's knee to shake her hand.

"You're welcome." Gratified by the effort the two of them were making to put on their best manners for her, Meg was filled with a sense of goodwill. Teaching was always satisfying to her, but their eagerness to please was a sign the summer would go especially well.

When the boy seemed to hesitate, Meg questioned, "Is there anything else, Dennis?"

His gaze slid uneasily toward his father, then back to her. "Do you think it would be okay for Dad to be there, too?"

Assuming that Dennis was just shy, she smiled at the boy. "Your father is welcome to join us if you would feel better with him there."

Dennis nodded. "I would." He looked back at his father, as if uncertain of his reaction.

Gavin's hesitation was evident. "I won't have any free time until the afternoon. Do you want to meet here at one?"

"Fine," Meg replied, wondering if she was imagining the undertones she sensed between father and son. The way they deliberately avoided looking at each other made her realize something was happening that she wasn't going to be privy to. She glanced at her watch. "Uh-oh. I'd better get going. I have to get into my costume."

Gavin stood up. "I'll walk you back."

"That's all right. You don't need to," she replied, sure that he just offered out of politeness. Gavin seemed intent on demonstrating good manners, which she appreciated, though she didn't think such formality necessary.

"But I *want* to," he said, looking directly into her eyes.

Her stomach did a little flip and she rose to her feet. "Well, okay then. I think I'd like you to walk me back."

Gavin blinked, as if surprised by her about-face. "You would?"

"Yes, I have a few questions to ask you."

He seemed disappointed. "Oh, rats. I thought you just wanted to be alone with me."

His outrageous statement threw Meg off balance. Flabbergasted, she wasn't sure how to reply. Her dismay must have shown, because Dennis tugged at his father's arm.

"Cut it out, Dad." He turned to Meg with an apologetic expression. "He just said that because he likes you."

Gavin's hand didn't muffle his son's mouth in time and Meg bit back a smile, tickled not only by Gavin's chagrined expression, but by the knowledge that her attraction to him wasn't one-sided.

His expression was bemused as he uncovered the boy's mouth. "Thanks a lot, Dennis." The boy just looked up in wide-eyed innocence and shrugged. Ruffling the child's hair, his father pushed him toward the kitchen. "Go put your dirty supper dishes away where they belong. I'll be back in a few minutes."

"Okay. Bye, Miss Harper."

"Goodbye, Dennis. I'll see you tomorrow."

Meg had a hard time suppressing her grin as Gavin glanced everywhere but at her as they walked back through the suffocating heat toward clown alley. He was obviously embarrassed about Dennis's comment, which gave him an air of vulnerability that she found endearing.

He cleared his throat as they emerged from the trailer area and began to cross the open backyard. "Did you want to ask me something?"

"Yes. I'm not familiar with the workings of the circus so far as the children are concerned. Who assists them during their lessons if the circus has no tutor?"

"Their parents."

"Oh. Have you taught him anything yet? Does he know the *ABC*'s or any letter sounds?"

Gavin's hesitation drew her attention and she studied him intently.

He colored and turned away. "He can sing the ABC song, but I'm not sure how much else he knows."

Meg thought his sudden discomfort odd and wondered if it had anything to do with the silent communication she'd intercepted back in the trailer between father and son.

"Well, then it's good that you'll be sitting in on Dennis's lessons. I think it's important for a parent to know what their child is doing. In your case it's even more so since you'll be taking up where I leave off." Meg acknowledged Gavin's nod with a smile, hoping her expression didn't reveal the ambivalent feelings warring within.

Professionally speaking, what Meg had said was true, but from a personal standpoint, she wasn't sure she'd be comfortable with Gavin's presence during the lessons. His bouts of male-female teasing disturbed her, even though she suspected the heart of a sincere man beat beneath Gavin's debonair image. Dennis's revelation that his father "liked" her meant that their relationship had definite possibilities, because she decided she "liked" Gavin, too. Seeing him with his son had shown her that there was more to this man than met the eye. The idea of something developing between them was both worrisome and exciting at the same time. A man who traveled constantly was hardly her ideal, no matter how worthwhile he was as an individual.

Gavin lifted his head abruptly, startling her from her introspection. "I forgot to ask how much you charge."

"Oh." She shrugged, considering her answer, then tilted her head and glanced at him sideways as a thought occurred. "If it's all right with you, I'd rather trade favors—horseback riding lessons for reading lessons. What do you say?"

Gavin smiled and took her hand as they stopped outside the clowns' changing tent. "You've got yourself a deal, teacher."

Meg shook on it. "Good. I've always loved horses, at least from afar. The opportunity to learn to ride never presented itself before. I can't think of a better time than now."

Before Meg could draw back her hand, Gavin covered it with his other one. "Meg." His voice dropped low and he gazed down with such intensity that she was riveted in place. "I just want to let you know that I appreciate you agreeing to tutor Dennis. Up until now I've never had much use for teachers, but I know how important it is for my son to learn to read. Having you get him started on the right track means a lot to me. I'm grateful that you're willing to take this on. Giving you riding instruction seems small compensation."

Meg inhaled slowly, sobered by the realization of how much he was depending on her. "I hope I live up to your expectations, Gavin."

His expression softened and she felt caressed by the warmth in his brown eyes. He squeezed her hand, then released it. "Don't worry, Meg. All these years of training horses has made me a pretty good judge of character. I know you're going to be good for Dennis."

"Does that mean horses are a lot like people, or that I'm a lot like a horse?" she asked with a crooked grin, pleased by his backhanded compliment.

He chuckled and rocked on his heels, studying her from beneath the brim of his Stetson. "As a matter of fact, your legs are as well shaped as any filly's I've ever seen."

Meg closed her eyes and shook her head. The touch of a finger under her chin startled her and her eyes flew open.

Gavin gently tilted her face up to his. "You know, Dennis was telling the truth before when he said I liked you. I do."

Meg's heart slammed against her ribs at his words. She was delighted, yet amazed that he'd admitted such a thing. Gavin obviously didn't believe in beating around the bush.

Willing to do her part in meeting the hand of friendship he'd extended, she answered, "Thank you. You're pretty nice yourself." She hoped he didn't notice the breathless quality of her voice. "And as far as teaching me to ride goes," she said more strongly, "I wouldn't sell myself short if I were you. Klutziness is part of my nature, which is why I'm a natural clown." Actually she was only clumsy when she got nervous, like when she was around a man she was attracted to, but he didn't need to know that.

He tilted his head, studying her. "I watched you during the first show. You're good."

Meg's heart soared. Gavin just jumped to the top of her favorite people list.

"But then," he continued in a serious tone, "that's not because of your klutziness. Don't kid a kidder, Meg. I've been around the circus long enough to know that a clown's klutziness takes lots of hours of practice. *Your* charisma comes from within. It's what's in your soul that people respond to." His voice took on a quiet, wondering quality. "You have very expressive eyes. Did you know? They tell what's in your heart."

If that was true, Meg was in big trouble, because right now she was feeling quite smitten with the man before her. And that's not what she wanted to feel for a man she'd just met, especially a man who traveled with a circus for a living.

As if Gavin also sensed that they were wading out of their depth, he reverted back to a teasing tone. "Of course, I like you better without the whiteface, but even with it, you're not bad. Maybe if I'd had a teacher as good-looking as you when I was young, I would have paid more attention to what was being drilled into my thick head."

Meg smiled, relieved by the lightened mood. "You're very generous with your compliments, but other than that, you seem to have come out all right, *especially* since you recognize a good thing when you see it," she teased.

Gavin's eyes widened in pretend shock. "Miss Harper, are you flirting with me? I could have sworn you said you didn't flirt."

Meg shook her head, amazed at herself. She was usually too painfully shy to flirt. How had this man provoked it?

"That must have slipped out because I have on Big Bertha's makeup," she replied, saying the first thing that popped into her head. "Flirting is second nature to her."

"Right." His tone was skeptical and she could tell he was having difficulty holding back a grin. "Want to try again?"

"No, I don't think so. I think I'd better just say goodbye before I put both my feet into my mouth." Meg nodded her head. "Good afternoon, Mr. Warner." Slipping through the tent flap, she beat a hasty retreat, but she could hear his laughter. Meg smiled. This was the second time that day she'd withdrawn from Gavin's presence with the sound of his amusement haunting her. It was amazing how one's perspective could change in a few short hours, though. The first time she'd been annoyed by his laughter. Now she felt caressed.

Meg inhaled deeply, her happy excitement adding a bounce to her step as she crossed to where her costume hung. Donning Big Bertha's clothes and wig, Meg rushed to gather her props and line up for the show, anxious to share her good spirits with the next audience.

Walking back to his trailer from clown alley, Gavin quickly lost the feeling of contentment being with Meg had brought about. He knew the time had come for him to have a talk with Dennis. The boy was beginning to notice things and ask questions that Gavin had been hoping he'd never have to face. He'd thought Nathan Marshall was the only person aware of his secret, but after hearing Dennis request his presence at the reading lessons, Gavin realized his son may have found him out.

The old feelings of shame and inadequacy that Gavin had thought he'd conquered rose and turned his gut to knots. Dread of facing Dennis with the truth slowed his steps. How in God's name was he going to explain to his son why he couldn't read?

Facing his trailer door, he gritted his teeth, knowing he'd put this off as long as he could. There was nothing left to do but tell Dennis his story and hope that the boy would still have a little respect left for his old man. Fear clutched at him as he entered the trailer.

"Dennis?"

"In here, Dad." The child's voice came from the direction of his bedroom.

Gavin strode down the short hall and stopped in his son's doorway, reluctant to utter the words he was afraid would forever change his relationship with his child. The boy was on his knees searching through his box of storybooks. A small stack of them lay on the blue rug next to the box.

"What are you doing?" Gavin asked.

"I'm getting out some of my books to show Miss Harper. Maybe she can teach me how to read them. I want to start with the toad and frog book. That's my favorite story."

Gavin gulped. "Uh, Dennis. When you learn to read the story, it may not be the same as when I told it to you." Gavin took off his Stetson, running his hand through his hair as his son looked up at him. "You see, I just made up a story to go with the pictures. I didn't read the actual words printed in the book."

Dennis sat back on his heels. His expression was serious. "Is that because you don't know how to read?"

The question hit Gavin with such force that he felt as if the wind had been knocked out of him. Swallowing hard, he stared down at his boots, unable to look his son in the eye. "I—" He choked on the word and tried again. "I didn't know you knew." Unsure of what he'd see in the boy's expression, Gavin slowly gazed upward. The silence seemed to stretch to eternity. The boy's frown was expected. His question wasn't.

"How come you look scared, Dad?"

Gavin tried to smile reassuringly. He knew it was his responsibility as a parent to be strong, but this was one time he failed miserably. "I guess it's because I *am* scared, Dennis," he admitted. "I'm afraid that you'll be ashamed of me now that you know."

"I'm not ashamed of you," the boy denied, and raised his arms to Gavin and asked, "Do you need a hug, Dad?"

Unable to answer around the lump in his throat, Gavin just nodded and raised his arms. Dennis jumped up and flew toward his father. Gavin bent, clutching his son to his chest.

Lowering himself onto the wooden rocking chair with Dennis snuggled on his lap, Gavin knew nothing had ever felt as good as his boy's arms around his neck at that moment.

They sat that way for several minutes, rocking slowly to and fro, son giving comfort to father, demonstrating his love without words, and Gavin realized something then that he'd never stopped to think about. In all his worry about Dennis's reaction, he hadn't considered that his son's love would be unconditional. It had been a long time since Gavin had experienced that special "no questions asked" type of love.

After several minutes of silence, Dennis lifted his head from his father's shoulder. "You know what, Dad? I bet Miss Harper could teach you to read, too."

Gavin looked into the young eyes so like his. "Is that why you asked Miss Harper if I could sit in on your lessons?"

Dennis nodded. "If you learn how to read, you won't have to go see Mr. Marshall when you get a letter from Uncle Henry and Aunt May." At Gavin's raised brows, the boy added, "I followed you one day and heard him read a letter to you. Are you mad?"

"No, I'm not mad."

"Then will you take reading lessons from Miss Harper with me?"

"No, Dennis, I don't think I can do that."

"How come?"

"I'd be too embarrassed if she found out I can't read. Please don't tell anyone else, either. Only Mr. Marshall knows, and I'd prefer it to stay that way."

"But Dad—"

Gavin interrupted his persistent son. "Listen, Dennis, I know it's hard for you to understand, but this is something I'm not proud of. I don't want people to think I'm stupid because I don't know how to read."

Dennis frowned. "Do you think I'm stupid 'cause I can't read?"

"No, of course not." Gavin hugged his son, then released him. "You're a little boy and just learning, but it's different when you're grown-up. People expect you to know more.''

Dennis's brow wrinkled in concentration, a sign that he was deep in thought, and Gavin wondered what his son would come up with next.

After a moment, the boy's expression brightened. ''Miss Harper said you could come to my reading lessons. Maybe if we didn't tell her you can't read, you could just sit and listen.''

Gavin shook his head. ''She's sure to think it's strange that I'm sitting there, Dennis. She probably thought you were bashful when she offered to have me stay during your lessons.''

''I could pretend I was bashful.'' Dennis's voice was hopeful.

''No, Dennis. It wouldn't be right. You know how I feel about dishonesty.'' Lying was something Gavin hated because he'd felt the need to resort to it so many times while he was growing up. Keeping his illiteracy a secret was a tremendous and difficult burden, and he didn't like having to lie to keep from being found out. He refused to let Dennis get caught in his web of deceit.

''Well, then maybe you could cook something while we sat at the kitchen table.''

''I don't know, Dennis.'' Gavin's lack of outright rejection was a mistake. The boy lit into the idea with an enthusiasm his father couldn't help but admire, even though Gavin knew it could spell his eventual doom.

''That would be a great idea, wouldn't it, Dad? You're always telling me that the reason you cook dinner here is because the meal they serve at the cook tent is too starchy. You don't want a nice lady like Miss Harper to have to eat that, do you?'' Dennis wiggled with excitement. ''You could cook dinner and listen while I had my lesson, and then we could all eat together afterward.''

*And then he could take Meg out for a riding lesson.* The unintentional thought startled Gavin and he flatly rejected the whole plan. Meg had obviously gotten under his skin already for him to even entertain the thought of having her at the dinner table every day. That setup sounded a little too cozy, and Gavin wasn't prepared to let any woman get that involved in his life.

"Sorry, Dennis. No way." He stood up and tossed his son over his shoulder like a sack of potatoes, effectively silencing any argument. "Come on. It's show time."

Gavin grabbed his Stetson and the smaller version that belonged to Dennis, then strode out of the trailer toward the horse tent. And if he hurried a little, he told himself that it was just because he didn't want *Dennis* to miss seeing Meg's walkaround routine.

# *Chapter Three*

Walking the short distance from her camper to Gavin's trailer at precisely one o'clock the next day, Meg apprehensively clutched a spiral notebook and some pencils to her bosom. She was unsure of what to expect from him on a personal level, so she decided to act as professionally as possible. She had a job to do. She couldn't let Gavin's presence distract her from her goal of teaching Dennis to read.

Rapping on the white door, she watched the undulating waves of heat shimmer off the surface of the metal roof. The combination of sun and lack of rain over the past two weeks had created dry conditions in the midwest, and animals and humans alike were becoming distressed by the unrelenting high temperatures. Meg was no exception. A trickle of sweat snaked unpleasantly down her stomach and she tried not to think of her centrally air-conditioned house back in Rockford.

The trailer door was yanked open by a bright-eyed Dennis in red shorts and striped T-shirt. He had a freshly scrubbed look and his normally unruly hair was as neat as a pin. Meg thought it sweet that he'd gotten all spiffed up for her.

"Hi! Come on in. Dad's not quite ready, but he'll be out in a minute. Do you want some lemonade?"

"I'd love some." Meg smiled and stepped into the trailer, following Dennis into the tiny, but well-equipped kitchen. A small oscillating fan on top of the white refrigerator stirred the air, providing a bit of relief, and Meg immediately turned her back to it and lifted her ponytail so the breeze could reach her neck. "Ahh," she sighed in delight.

Dennis boosted himself up and knelt on the counter to reach the cabinet with the glasses.

"Can I help you with that?" she asked.

"No, I can do it. You can sit down if you want. Dad said we should work at the table."

"Okay." Meg would give herself a few more seconds in front of the fan, though. How she missed her creature comforts!

Gavin strode into the kitchen as Dennis finished pouring the liquid into three glasses. "Just in time, I see. Thanks, Dennis." He picked up two glasses, handing one to Meg. "Hi."

How could a man infuse so much charm into one little word? Gavin's brown eyes sparkled with warmth and his voice was as smooth as pure honey. Meg had always been partial to honey.

"Hi," she murmured, taking the glass from his hand. He had a fresh-from-the-shower, clean, soapy smell and his still-wet hair had just been combed. He wore khaki safari-type shorts, a white cotton knit shirt and brown deck shoes. Wow. Meg had never seen such great legs on a man before. They were long, lean and lightly sprinkled with hair. Gavin's whole physique was that of a man in his prime. He was muscular, but not overly so, and he didn't have an extra ounce of fat on him. The man packed quite a wallop.

Coming to her senses, she thanked Dennis for the lemonade and sat down at the square wooden table. "Perhaps we should get started. Dennis, why don't you sit here next to me?'' That left Gavin in the chair opposite hers, which would be fine if she didn't look up. Meg opened the spiral notebook. On the first page she had printed the alphabet and a list of short, high-frequency words. On the next page, she had printed a list of simple, three-letter words, using different vowels and consonants, and then longer words with blends. Starting at the beginning, she went through them with Dennis, asking him to identify letters and their sounds, then seeing if he could recognize the short, high-frequency words. She asked him to pronounce what he could so she would be able to determine his skill level.

Once Meg had decided on an appropriate starting point, she explained to Dennis and his father that she would be teaching an intensive phonics method. She'd been teaching it for the past three years to her first-graders back in Rockford, and thought that since she was working one-on-one with Dennis, they'd be able to progress more quickly through the program than the six months it normally took.

Meg looked at Gavin. ''If you could practice what we go over with Dennis before he goes to bed, that would help reinforce the information so he can grasp it that much faster.''

Gavin's breath caught in his throat and a tightness gripped his chest. He just hoped he didn't look as stunned as he felt. God, he'd known this wouldn't work.

''Dad doesn't have time to go over this stuff when he puts me to bed.'' Dennis's voice rose above the sound of blood pounding in Gavin's ears and he focused on what his son was saying.

''I go to bed right after our Wild West act in the second show, but Dad has to change for his equestrian act.''

''Oh.'' Meg paused. ''Do you stay here all by yourself until the big top's down?''

''No. Rico's grandma comes and checks on me. That's why we always park our trailer right next to theirs.'' Dennis looked up at him. ''Right, Dad?''

Gavin's heart swelled with gratitude as he smiled down at his son. Dennis had understood the panic he'd been in and had come to his rescue. Gavin didn't know what he'd ever done to deserve Dennis, but he thanked God he'd been so richly blessed.

"Right." Gavin gently squeezed the boy's shoulder and stood up, unable to face the possibility of being drawn into the reading lesson and asked to perform some other task of which he was incapable. "It's time for me to start cooking dinner. You two go on about your business. I'll try not to bother you."

He turned his back on Meg and Dennis and dug through the refrigerator, pulling out what he'd need. His self-esteem had just taken a tremendous blow and Gavin felt driven to redeem himself in some way. He'd always found cooking to be satisfying, so threw himself into preparing a meal he could be proud of.

While he skinned chicken breasts and chopped vegetables, Gavin listened to the conversation going on at the table. Meg was explaining something about vowels, consonants and guardians to Dennis. Although Gavin had absolutely no idea what she was talking about, he enjoyed listening to her sweet, melodic voice and watching the way her mouth formed the letter sounds. She smiled a lot, encouraging Dennis, and he could tell his son was enjoying the lesson.

Gavin noticed that Meg never scolded Dennis when he made a mistake, but gently corrected him instead. She earned Gavin's respect for that.

Gavin wondered if things might have been different for him if he'd had a kind, patient teacher like Meg. Maybe then he could have figured out the trick to reading. Of course, he would have needed several teachers like her in a row since he'd never attended any school for more than three months at a time. The majority of his teachers had considered him a discipline problem and hadn't known what to do with him when he refused to read or write, but merely sat with his arms folded stubbornly.

Gavin had listened, and he'd learned. Math and science had been his favorite subjects, and he'd been good at them.

But he'd never unraveled the mystery of reading. Most of the teachers had given up on him, since they knew he wouldn't be around long, but when his mother died when he was thirteen, Gavin's whole life had changed.

He went to live with his aunt and uncle in a small town in Kentucky. That's when he learned to live by his charm and wits to avoid doing his schoolwork. More often than not he paid some other kid to do his homework for him with the money he earned working around his uncle's horse farm. Math wasn't a problem for him and he'd actually done passably well in guessing answers on multiple choice tests. He'd ditched the essay tests, but few teachers gave him trouble.

The gossips in the small town had spread word of his poor and neglected childhood, how his mother, a nightclub singer, had dragged him around the country with her. Everyone knew that Henry and May Warner were trying their best to civilize the wild teenager they'd inherited, and Gavin's teachers hadn't wanted to add to their burden.

So, he'd drifted through high school, learning by listening, but lacking the skills to demonstrate what he knew. The day he discovered he wouldn't be graduating with the rest of the senior class he'd been so ashamed that he knew he had no choice but to run away from home. He'd learned to love his Aunt May and Uncle Henry too much to bear the pain and disappointment he knew would be in their eyes when they found out. That was the day he'd joined the Nathan Marshall Circus.

Gavin shook off his old memories and listened to the conversation going on behind him, determined that his son would learn to read, no matter what the cost.

"No, Dennis," Meg said. "That's not quite right. Look back at these two words. Which one has the short *i* sound in it?" She patiently repeated the same thing he'd heard her say to Dennis three times already.

"It."

"Right. Now read the short *e* word."

"Egg."

"Can you hear the difference in the sounds they make?"

Gavin glanced over his shoulder and saw Dennis nod his head. His son had obviously picked up a few of the fundamentals from hanging around his friend Rico during his lessons. Rico was seven and had been enrolled in correspondence school for a year. Since his parents and grandparents were with the circus, Rico had plenty of people to teach him.

Gavin frowned. If he enrolled Dennis in the correspondence school, he'd have to find someone else to teach his son. God knew he couldn't.

"Okay, now try this word." Meg pointed to the paper with one long slim finger.

"Bell."

"Good boy, but I'll bet I can trick you with the next one," she teased. "Watch out."

His son grinned. "Oh, no, you won't." Taking up the challenge, Dennis stared hard at the word. "It's . . . win!"

"Right. You win!" Meg patted the boy's back.

Gavin smiled, acknowledging that Meg certainly had a gift for making learning fun. She was obviously smart, too. She'd written down all the reading lessons from memory without having any of her workbooks to guide her. He'd have to watch himself around her. He had a feeling she wouldn't miss a clue if he accidentally slipped up and somehow let on that he couldn't read.

As Gavin browned the chicken and stirred biscuit batter, he found his gaze wandering over Meg's profile. Her ponytail bounced sassily when she moved her head, emphasizing the graceful curve of her slender neck as she bent over the notebook. Her high cheekbones tapered down to a slightly pointed chin, and she had a narrow nose and thin, arching eyebrows, which were slightly darker than her chestnut-colored hair. As was common to redheads, her skin was pale, translucent, and not a bit tan. He could tell she'd gotten a little too much sun lately by the red border revealed along her scooped neckline. Her features had a fine-boned fragility about them that were utterly feminine and very appealing. Gavin liked what he saw and would have invited her to dinner if she'd been anyone other than who she was. Courting a teacher would be courting trouble.

"I thought you said you'd try not to bother us." Meg's voice startled Gavin as he was removing a tray of biscuits from the oven.

"I'm sorry. What did I do?" he asked, hoping she hadn't caught him staring.

"You created smells that are driving Dennis and me wild." Her reply relieved and delighted him. "What is that you're cooking?" she asked.

"Chicken Zucchini." Gavin slid a pan of brownie batter into the hot oven. He'd made Dennis's favorite dessert as a way of saying thank-you.

The child's eyes lit up when he spied the pan. "Oh, boy. Brownies!"

"Not unless you eat all your vegetables," Gavin admonished.

Meg sniffed delicately. "I smell garlic."

"Right." He stirred the mixture in the frying pan. "Besides chicken and zucchini, the other ingredients are onions, water chestnuts, and bamboo shoots. I serve it over rice." He knew he couldn't get away with not inviting her to dinner the second he saw the longing expression in her blue-green eyes. "There's enough for three."

She blushed a pretty shade of pink and dropped her gaze. "Thank you, but I didn't mean to invite myself. Besides, Carol is probably expecting me to meet her for dinner at the cook tent."

Gavin was surprised at Meg's return to shyness. She'd been relaxed and at ease with Dennis during the lesson. Gavin wished she could feel as comfortable with him as she did with his son, but decided it was probably best for him if she didn't.

Meg closed the spiral notebook and stood up. "You did a good job today, Dennis. I'll see you tomorrow."

"Okay. Bye, Miss Harper."

Gavin turned off the stove. "Dennis, go wash up and start setting the table, please. We'll be eating in a few minutes. I'll walk Miss Harper to the door."

He followed Meg, noticing that her movement was slightly stiff. "Are you up to having a riding lesson today? You look like you're in pain."

She stopped and turned. Her smile was sheepish. "I'm afraid that I'm not used to the rigors of setting up the big top." She lifted her palm, as if to take an oath. "*But*, I *will* get into shape this summer."

Gavin grinned and glanced down the length of her. "Oh, I don't know. Your shape already looks pretty good to me."

Meg rolled her eyes. "You're outrageous." But her blush gave away that she wasn't unaffected by the compliment.

Gavin chuckled. He enjoyed teasing her out of her shyness.

"If you're still game, meet me at the horse tent at three o'clock," he said, pleased that she wasn't going to call off their time together. "I know it's hot, but you'd better change into jeans and boots if you have them."

She frowned. "I don't have any boots. Would gym shoes be okay?"

"Not really. Do you have something with a hard heel?"

"My loafers."

He nodded. "Those will do. You'd better wear something to protect that delicate skin of yours, too."

"I have sunscreen."

"Well be sure to put plenty on," he said gruffly, not relishing the thought of her being burned by the blistering sun.

"Okay. Bye." Her shy smile made Gavin's heart turn over. God help him, he couldn't wait until he was with her again, teacher or not.

Meg arrived at the horse tent early, anxious to begin her lesson, or so she had told herself. The fact that her insides turned to mush the moment she spotted Gavin hefting a large saddle onto the back of a dappled gray horse had very little to do with the horse and a lot to do with the man.

He turned at her approach, and the smile that spread across his features made her heart beat faster, for it wasn't just on his face. It was in his eyes, those gorgeous brown eyes that were perpetually shaded by a Stetson. She noted that he'd changed from shorts into his standard outfit of jeans, T-shirt, and boots. This time his shirt was yellow, though, a very becoming color that showed off his tanned face and arms.

"Hi, Meg. Meet Misty. She'll be your mount until you're ready to advance to something beyond slow and deliberate." Gavin reached under the horse and tightened the strap that extended under its belly.

Saddling horses was obviously second nature to Gavin, since he showed no fear at getting up close and personal with the creature. But Meg's eyes widened as she took a good look at Misty. My gosh, she'd realized horses were big, but she'd never been up close enough to discover how *overwhelmingly* big. *And* powerful. Just standing next to the large beast threatened her composure, and she bit her lip to keep from chickening out.

Swallowing nervously, she patted the horse's neck. "I think Misty will be just fine." She hoped the beast would respond to her vote of confidence. She'd always heard that animals could sense when people were afraid of them, so she tried to bluff with a positive attitude. "Hello, girl."

Gavin straightened up. "Ready for your first lesson?"

"As ready as I'll ever be," Meg replied, proud that her voice didn't quaver. "Just remember that I know absolutely nothing about horses."

"Gotcha." He fastened the horse's bridle, then turned her way and handed her a hard hat. "Here. Put this on."

She looked it over. "What's this? My crash helmet?" Placing it on her head, she fastened the strap under her chin. "It's awfully warm. Do you really think I need it?"

"Yes. We can't have you getting a crack in that pretty head of yours now, can we?"

"Hopefully not," she answered wryly.

"All right, we'll start out with mounting. I'll hold the reins until you get the hang of it. Now, grab the saddle horn with your left hand and slip your left foot into the stirrup. You want to pull yourself up and throw your right leg over. Got that?"

"Yes. I've seen how it's done in cowboy movies." Meg figured the maneuver would be a piece of cake, but she hadn't counted on her center of balance being so low and the horse being so high. Her little hop wasn't nearly enough to boost her all the way up and over, so she hung in midair with her rear end sticking out one way and her right leg jutting out at an awkward angle the other way. Knowing she must look absolutely ridiculous, she lowered her right leg to the ground and concentrated on maintaining her balance with her left foot still in the stirrup.

She glanced at Gavin over her shoulder and muttered, "Not as easy as it looks, is it?" She knew she was blushing furiously and was grateful that he had the sensitivity not to laugh.

He nodded. "Try again."

This time she put forth more effort and made it, swinging her leg over as he'd instructed and landing with a plop in the saddle. Pleased by her achievement, she glanced down for Gavin's approval, then gulped and sat perfectly still. Boy, he was a long way down.

"Not too bad," he said, "but next time don't land so hard in the saddle." He reached for her leg. "Take your foot out of the stirrup for a second so I can adjust it."

"Do I have to?" she asked, clutching the saddle horn. This was a lot scarier than she'd thought it would be.

Gavin chuckled. "Yes, you do, unless you want to lose your stirrup later and take the chance of falling off."

Meg kicked her foot free and Gavin adjusted the strap. He replaced her foot and rubbed her jean-covered calf when he was done.

"Don't worry, Meg. I won't let anything happen to you. Just try to relax."

Relax? He had to be kidding. She managed a sickly smile and waited for him to adjust her other stirrup. Learning to ride wasn't going to be nearly as simple as she'd originally thought. She wasn't sure it was going to be as fun, either, but how could she back out now without looking foolish? She swallowed hard. She knew she'd have to make the best of it. She refused to be a coward in front of Gavin.

Gavin backed Misty away from the line of tethered horses and handed Meg the reins. "Hold them in your left hand like this. Now sit tight. I'll be right back."

"You're leaving me?" Wide-eyed, she held her breath, hoping that if she didn't move, the horse wouldn't, either.

"I'm just getting Ginger, my horse."

She heard the creak of leather behind her, but didn't dare turn her head as her horse suddenly shifted beneath her. Meg's heart jumped into her throat. "Whoa, Misty."

Gavin rode up and stopped next to her. He was seated atop the chestnut mare she'd seen him riding during the shows. She immediately reached out her right hand to him. He caught it in his.

"Misty moved and I didn't know what to do."

"I'm sorry you were frightened." He squeezed her hand. "Misty was just shifting her weight. She wasn't going anywhere."

Meg felt foolish for overreacting and cautiously glanced sideways. "This is much scarier than I'd imagined it would be. I feel like I don't have any control." She grimaced. "It's sort of like driving a bus without a steering wheel or brake pedal."

"My fault. I guess I should have checked you out as soon as you mounted. You do have control, Meg. The reins are your steering wheel and brake pedal." He demonstrated. "Shift them this way if you want to go right, the opposite way to go left, and pull back on them firmly to stop. It's really very easy. Any questions?"

"Where's Misty's gas pedal?"

His brown eyes lit up. "Are you sure you're ready for that?" he teased. "I thought maybe you'd rather stand here holding hands all afternoon."

She immediately let go of him and returned to gripping the saddle horn instead. "Funny," she muttered.

Gavin shrugged. "Okay, to make her move, all you have to do is squeeze your legs and kick your heels into her sides. And relax your death grip on that horn." He reached over and brushed her hand away. "You shouldn't have to hold on to it. Just loosen up and rest your hand on your lap."

Properly chastised, meekly Meg did as he said.

"Now sit up straight and keep your heels down. Only the balls of your feet should be in the stirrup. Your ankles are going to act as your shock absorbers."

Meg smiled, pleased that he'd tailored his language so she could understand. She followed his directions and felt fairly stable. Maybe she was getting her balance.

"There, that's better." Gavin nudged his horse forward. "Now, follow my lead. We're going to go for a nice slow walk through the field on the other side of the cook tent." He turned in his saddle to watch her.

Meg gently kicked her heels into Misty's side and the horse stepped lively, following Ginger. "Hey, I did it." She couldn't have been more surprised.

Gavin just said, "Good girl," effectively squelching Meg's inclination to grab hold of the saddle horn again now that she was moving. The urge to please him was strong.

They walked through the backyard without mishap and Meg thought perhaps riding wouldn't be so bad after all. A small group of roustabouts emerged from the cook tent just as she and Gavin were skirting it and one of the men jumped back so fast that he spilled hot coffee down his leg.

"Ouch! Dammit all!" His loud gruff voice startled Meg, who automatically pulled back on Misty's reins.

Unfortunately the man's shout had also startled her horse. Misty's high-pitched neigh turned Meg's blood to ice water. She froze as her horse rolled her eyes and shied back, away from the roustabout. Prancing skittishly, Misty tossed her head back and Meg was almost jostled right out of the saddle. Feeling utterly helpless, she grabbed the saddle horn with both hands and held on for dear life.

Suddenly Gavin was there, still atop his horse. He grabbed the reins from Meg's stiff fingers.

"Hold on!" he commanded, then turned his horse and led her and Misty out of harm's way.

"You okay?" Gavin asked once they stopped out in the middle of the open field.

"Yes, thanks to you. That was a little hairy for a minute, though. I feel like I should be wearing a big yellow sign that says Student Driver."

Meg didn't know if what she'd said was really that funny, or whether Gavin was just laughing in relief, but his amusement grew from down deep as he threw back his head and let it boom forth. She grinned, just watching him, until he calmed down and looked at her.

"You're something else, Meg. Five minutes ago you were quaking in your boots standing still, and now, *after* you almost get thrown, you sit there and make jokes. If I wasn't afraid I'd unseat you, I'd give you a big kiss."

Well that was certainly something to make her pulse leap. If she'd been a braver woman, she would have told Gavin that his kiss might be worth falling off a horse, but of course, she couldn't. She shrugged instead. "You seemed to have the situation well in hand, and frankly, it all happened so fast that it was over before I had a chance to react."

He grabbed her hand and shook his head in self-deprecation. "God, great teacher I would have turned out to be if you'd been thrown."

"Gavin, don't worry about it. It's over and I'm fine. You certainly have nothing to feel guilty about. Your quick action was what saved me from whatever could have happened. Thank you for being there when I needed you." Meg could read in Gavin's eyes that he appreciated hearing that from her and a heartrending tenderness for him swelled within her breast. The tight clasp of her hand in his didn't seem enough to reflect the poignancy of the moment, and by the look of intense desire burning in Gavin's eyes, she didn't think it was enough for him, either.

As if drawn together magnetically, they each began to lean toward the other, but then Gavin stopped. He squeezed her hand before letting go of it, but the gesture was small consolation to Meg. She wondered what had changed his mind.

Gavin rode a few steps ahead and turned his horse to face her. His mouth was set in a grim line, which indicated to Meg that he was reining in his emotions as well as Ginger, who was prancing around like she wanted a good run.

"Okay, Meg, I want you to try to ride around me. You're going to have to learn how to turn her if you want control. Take it slow and easy and move the reins like I showed you."

She respected Gavin's wishes. He was out here to teach her to ride and she was out here to learn. That was the deal they'd made and he was keeping up his end of it. So why was she so disappointed that he was acting like an instructor?

# Chapter Four

Meg was exhausted. And sore. Muscles she hadn't used in years, if ever, complained of their existence. And this was only her fourth day with the circus. She wasn't sure she'd survive the next ten weeks!

Standing in the tiny shower stall of the camper, she longed for the spacious shower at home, where she could have adjusted the water temperature and massage nozzle to soothe her aching muscles for as long as she wanted.

Taking down the big top and folding it after the final show, then setting it up forty or so miles away at five-thirty every morning was not Meg's idea of fun. She *did* experience a rather awesome sense of accomplishment as well as a sense of camaraderie with her fellow workers once the job was done. Unfortunately her rebellious muscles negated those positive feelings.

Someone knocked on the camper door just as Meg finished toweling herself dry. She wrapped the towel firmly around her torso and stood behind the door as she opened it a few inches. Peering out, she looked down at the masculine form in navy T-shirt, faded jeans and boots, who was standing in the bright sunlight.

Gavin's eyes lit up when he saw her. "Hi."

Remembering her wet, stringy hair and lack of makeup, Meg pulled back into the camper's shadowy interior as best she could. "Hi."

"I brought you some liniment to put on your sore muscles." He held out a brown bottle.

"How considerate! Thank you." She stretched out a bare arm and took the bottle from his hand. "How did you know I needed this?"

Gavin's speculative look caused a hot blush to spread over her body and she retreated back again into the shadows.

He smiled. "You were bound to. Yesterday was the first time you'd ever set up the big top or ridden horseback." He tipped back his Stetson, revealing more of his eyes. "Besides, I saw you flinching when you were lacing the canvas this morning."

She smiled in chagrin. "I didn't realize I was that obvious."

He hooked his thumbs onto his belt and shrugged. "You probably weren't to most people, but I seem to have developed radar where you're concerned."

Flattered, Meg glanced down and unscrewed the cap from the glass bottle in her hand.

"I hope this works." She took a whiff of the liniment and grimaced. "Whew!"

He chuckled and her gaze darted to his twinkling brown eyes.

"You don't really expect me to use this stinky stuff, do you?" She'd need a clothespin for her nose if she did.

"Sure. Why not?"

She wrinkled her nose and screwed the cap back on. "I want to make friends, not drive them away."

He reached for the bottle and frowned. "This is no time for vanity. Besides, you won't smell any different than a lot of other people around here." He removed the cap and handed the liniment back to her. "Use it or I'll come in there and put it on you myself."

Meg's heart skipped a beat at his determined tone. Grabbing the bottle and cap with one hand, she nervously tugged the towel higher on her breasts with the other.

"I'll do it myself, thank you," she replied, disturbed by the shiver of awareness that skittered through her. Standing half-naked with only a door separating her from Gavin obviously wasn't very sensible.

"I . . . I'd better get dressed now," she stammered. "I'll see you this afternoon." Meg shut the door, hoping her abruptness didn't appear rude. With her skin still tingling, she quickly slipped into her lavender shorts outfit.

The muffled rumble of Gavin's voice outside was followed by Carol's laughter, and when Carol stepped into the camper a minute later, Meg's curiosity got the best of her.

"What did Gavin say that was so funny?" Meg asked as casually as she could. Seated at the small table, she avoided her friend's gaze as she combed the tangles from her wet, shoulder-length hair.

Carol took the seat across from her and tossed a newspaper down onto the table. "I'm not sure I should tell you. It was pretty risqué."

Meg looked up. "Risqué?" Gavin was making risqué comments to Carol? The unexpected flash of jealousy surprised her. "Then you have to tell me."

Carol shook her head. "Frankly I think that man has the hots for you."

Meg's eyes widened. "Why?"

"He said, and I quote, 'Tell Meg that if she's still sore later, I'd be happy to give her a backrub.' And then he zapped me with this hungry, sexy smile that practically melted my tennis shoes."

Meg covered her mouth with her palm to hide the smile that sprang to her lips.

Carol folded her arms primly. "Looks like a little more went on yesterday between you two than you said, doesn't it?"

Meg chose to ignore her and picked up the brown bottle. "What's that?" Carol asked.

"Liniment. Gavin brought it by for my sore muscles."

Carol propped an elbow on the table and leaned her cheek against her fist. "It's disgusting that you're being rewarded for not exercising."

Meg raised her eyebrows. "Sore muscles are a reward?"

Carol's sigh was audible. "No, but a gorgeous hunk bringing you liniment and offering to give you a massage certainly is. Maybe I should cancel my membership at the health club." She raised her nose in the air and sniffed. "Hey, that stinks."

Meg smiled wryly. "Tell me about it. Are you sure you wouldn't like to reconsider?" She poured a small amount of the liquid onto her fingertips and rubbed it into her upper arm and shoulder.

Carol leaned back. "Holy cats! I think I'll go read the newspaper outside. Let me know when you're ready to go to breakfast."

Feeling conspicuously stinky, Meg tried to stay downwind of Carol as they walked to the trailer known as the cook house. She picked up her tray of eggs, bacon, oatmeal and coffee and then stood beside her friend looking around for empty table space in the crowded tent.

"Miss Harper!" a child's voice called.

She turned to see Dennis standing and waving. Seated next to the boy, Gavin looked up and caught her eye. His lips slowly curved upward as he beckoned to them and Meg's pulse quickened. Determined not to let her self-consciousness show, she held her head high.

Carol nodded toward Gavin's table, which was on the other side of the tent. "You lead the way. That liniment you've got on could part the Red Sea. It's bound to help now."

Meg tossed her friend a dirty look, but Carol just grinned. Meg squeezed through the benches of show people, grateful that no one seemed to notice her unappealing scent.

Gavin stood beside Dennis when she and Carol reached the table, even though none of the other men seemed so inclined.

"Hi, Miss Harper!" Dennis said with bubbly enthusiasm. "You and your friend can sit across from me and Dad."

Meg smiled at the grinning boy. "Thanks, Dennis." She set down her tray and the folded newspaper she had under her arm, then slipped her legs through the opening on the picnic-styled table and carefully sat down on her tender posterior.

"Are you feeling better, Miss Harper?" Dennis asked. "Did that liniment Dad gave you help?"

Meg's eyes shifted quickly from the boy to the man watching her over the rim of his coffee cup.

"Yes, I am feeling a little better now. Thank you for asking, Dennis." She wasn't about to admit that her well-being stemmed mostly from the boost of adrenaline his father's presence had produced.

She introduced Dennis to Carol, then dug into her oatmeal. Right now food was a much higher priority than conversation. Meg had risen before dawn and devoted four hours to setting up the big top. She was hungry!

Gavin introduced them to a few individuals and settled for waving a greeting to others within the large tent. He clearly knew everyone, but all during the meal Meg could feel his attention centered on her. She kept catching him staring. Coward that she was, she'd glance away first every time, but her gaze returned to him whenever she thought he wasn't looking.

The tension inside her wound tighter and tighter and she became aware of Gavin's slightest move and expression. She noticed the small things, like the way his right thumb idly skimmed up and down the coffee mug's handle when he was listening to someone and the way he cocked one eyebrow higher than the other when he thought someone was telling a fish tale.

She especially noted the way he treated Dennis. Gavin listened to the boy as patiently as he listened to what the adults had to say, and when Dennis made a bad pun, he groaned as loudly as everyone else, but then gave his son an affectionate hug afterward. It was as if Gavin wanted to reassure Dennis that he was worthwhile, even if his comment was lacking. Meg felt a warm glow flow through her.

Dennis was the first to leave the table, running off to play with his friend Rico. Then the people seated around them began to leave, until only Carol, Gavin and Meg were left. Gavin offered to get them all another cup of coffee, but Carol refused, saying that she had some things to wash out. Meg knew differently and was embarrassed by her friend's obvious ploy to leave her and Gavin alone together.

"I'll go with you, Carol." Meg began to rise, but Gavin reached out and covered her hand with his.

"Meg, wait. I want to talk to you about something. Could you stay for a few more minutes?"

She hesitated, then sat down. "Sure."

"See you later." Carol winked at Meg and strolled out of the tent.

Meg waited as Gavin withdrew his hand from hers and got up to refill their coffee mugs. Returning to the table, he smiled as he sat across from her. "I wasn't sure if you'd use the liniment."

She raised her eyebrows. "I recall that you didn't leave me much of a choice."

He shook his head and grinned unrepentantly. "That was all a bluff, though I do think you'll be glad you used it." He set down his cup, folded his arms on the table and leaned toward her. His brown eyes captured hers. "I brought it by as an excuse to see you."

The intimate message made her breathless. A soft "Oh" was the best she could manage as his implication was clear. Gavin *was* interested in her, and not just as his son's teacher. The problem was, her inexperience in dealing with men on a personal level made her unable to volley the ball Gavin had just lobbed into her court. She groped for an appropriate reply, stalling for time by pretending to be distracted by a raucous trio of roustabouts.

Gavin cringed inwardly when Meg didn't say anything. What was worse, she was looking everywhere but at him. Maybe she thought he was coming on too strong. He probably was. God knows, ever since he'd walked her back to clown alley two days ago, he'd been feeling like an adolescent with a crush. Bewitched, that's what he was. All morning he'd kept reliving their horseback ride together when he should have been concentrating on raising the big top. And when he'd tried to catch a glimpse of her, the guys kidded him about being preoccupied. He'd told them he hadn't slept well, which was the truth, but Jacques, the lion tamer, hadn't believed him.

"Only a woman can distract a man so thoroughly," he'd said to Gavin in his thick French accent. "I know. My Monique's been distracting me for twenty years."

"So what do you do about it?" Gavin had asked.

His friend had replied, "Do? There's nothing to do, *mon ami*. Fight a woman's power? Bah!" He'd thrown up his hands. "A waste of time! Me, I enjoy." With a twinkle in his eye, he'd leaned close to Gavin and whispered conspiratorially, "And if ze truth be told, I think maybe I distract my Monique a little bit myself."

Bowing to experience, Gavin had followed his friend's advice, but now he wasn't so sure he'd done the right thing. Meg was so shy. His boldness had probably scared her off, or else—he was jolted by another thought—maybe she had a boyfriend.

"Are you dating anyone at home?" he asked. He believed in being direct.

Her blue-eyed gaze flew back to his and a startled "No" burst from her lips.

Relieved, he asked, "Then would you like to go someplace tomorrow? We'll have the whole day to ourselves once I feed the horses in the morning."

Her smile was slow, but genuine. "I'd like that. But what about Dennis?"

"He's going fishing with Rico and his grandfather. They're going to make a day of it."

"Oh. Are you sure you wouldn't rather go with them?"

Gavin sat back, baffled. She'd just told him she'd like to spend the day with him. Was she changing her mind already?

"I mean . . ." She paused, and he saw a blush pinken her cheeks. "If you'd rather fish, I'd understand. I . . . I don't want you to feel that you're obligated to give me a riding lesson, or anything."

He leaned toward her. "Meg, first of all, besides hating to fish, I wouldn't dream of intruding on the boys' day with Joe Cannone. Joe's like Dennis's grandfather as well as Rico's, and their time spent fishing together is sacred."

"Oh. That's nice."

"Yes, it is nice, and *so are you*," he emphasized, "which brings me to my second point. I don't feel obligated to give you a lesson, though I certainly wouldn't mind spending part of the day riding. I just want to be with you, and I don't much care what we do together. You're an attractive woman and I'd like to get to know you better. Understand?"

Her lips quivered with a wisp of a smile and the bright sparkle in her blue eyes sent an arrow right through his heart. "Thank you. I'm flattered."

Meg had to be the most modest woman he'd ever met, Gavin decided. The outgoing show women he knew would have thrown back some kind of brazen line about wanting to get to know him better, too.

He smiled. "We can decide where we want to go later. You probably have something else to do right now."

"Not really. I was just going to read the newspaper." She held it out. "Would you like to share?"

Her innocent question hit Gavin like a punch in the stomach. Reality crashed down around him and chased away the daydream he'd been living in all morning.

"No. No thanks, Meg. I have to get to work. I'll see you this afternoon."

Gavin left the cook tent cursing himself for a fool. No matter how Meg attracted him, he should have fought her allure and never made a date with her. They were too different. God, an illiterate and a teacher. What could he have been thinking of?

Meg watched Gavin leave the tent, curious as to why he'd asked her out after she'd acted like such a dolt. She certainly hadn't dazzled him with sparkling conversation. And when he'd made a pass, she'd been stricken dumb. No doubt about it, she was a zero when it came to interpersonal relationships. Would she never outgrow this irritating shyness?

She was an adult now, no longer that introverted child who'd never lived in one place long enough to develop friendships. Meg had traveled the world, but she'd been very sheltered and had filled the void in her social life with books. She'd finally learned to make conversation when she'd attended a private girls' high school and then a small women's college. But she'd never felt comfortable talking to strangers, especially men. Even now, she had few friends and rarely dated. Meg knew she lacked the self-confidence that would allow her to relax and be herself. That was one of the reasons she enjoyed portraying her clown character so much. She didn't feel inhibited as Big Bertha.

Meg sighed. Too bad she hadn't worn her whiteface to breakfast. Maybe then she would have been able to think of something to say.

Later that afternoon during Dennis's reading lesson, Meg surreptitiously watched Gavin. He was seated across from her with a small stack of mending piled before him. He sewed on a few buttons and restitched a length of fringe that had come loose from Dennis's cowboy costume. The man was a domestic wonder. He even darned socks!

After the lesson, Dennis ran out to play and Meg couldn't resist questioning Gavin.

"Who taught you to sew?" she asked, examining one of Dennis's socks.

Gavin looked up. "Hmm? Oh, my aunt. Aunt May was a feminist long before it was fashionable. She believed that all men should be able to take care of themselves."

Meg smiled. "Good for her. Did she teach you to cook, too?" The aroma of the beef stew simmering on the stove had been making Meg's mouth water for the past hour.

Gavin's brow puckered in the same appealing way as Dennis's when he was thinking about something.

"Let's just say that Aunt May taught me to cook *well*," he replied. "Until I moved in with her and Uncle Henry, most of what I cooked came out of cans."

"Oh." Meg's face must have revealed her repugnance, because Gavin laughed.

"Disgusting, isn't it? Oh course, I was just a kid then and didn't know any better."

"Well, you've certainly improved if what you cook tastes as good as it smells. Would you mind sharing your recipe, or is it an old family secret?"

"It's no secret, but I don't follow a recipe. I just throw in a little of this and a little of that. You can watch the next time I make it. That's how I learned to cook. My aunt was big on 'hands on' experience." He held out his palms. "I think I was the only guy in high school with dishpan hands."

Meg laughed and he went on.

"Laundry, housekeeping, mending..." He held up the needle and thread. "Aunt May taught it all."

"Well, you were a good student. You obviously learned a lot."

The glint in Gavin's eyes told her he was surprised by the compliment. "Thanks, but it's probably more that my aunt was a good teacher."

"Or perhaps both," she added.

He smiled and shrugged. "Maybe."

Meg liked that. She hadn't met many men willing to give credit to the women who'd been positive influences in their lives.

"Your aunt sounds like a wonderful person. You're obviously fond of her."

"Yeah, she's a sweetheart."

"Do you mind if I ask why you lived with your aunt and uncle?"

Gavin frowned as he bit off a thread and placed the sock he'd been mending on top of the pile.

"I'm sorry," Meg quickly interjected. "That was nosy of me. You don't have to answer that. I shouldn't have asked."

Gavin looked up at Meg in surprise, dismayed that she'd suddenly turned into the shy, nervous bunny rabbit she'd been at breakfast. Ordinarily he didn't care to discuss very much of his past, but right now he was more concerned with recapturing their easy flow of conversation.

"It's all right, Meg. I don't mind telling you." He was glad to see her settle back on the kitchen chair. She no longer looked ready to take flight.

"My father died somewhere in Vietnam when I was four. I really don't remember him. I lived with my mom until she became ill. She died not long after my thirteenth birthday. So, Aunt May and Uncle Henry took me in."

"I'm sorry." The sympathetic expression in her eyes touched his heart.

He shook his head, dispelling the soft feeling she had created. "No, that's all right. It was a long time ago." He stuck the needle into a small red pincushion and tossed it into a wicker basket. Tipping his chair back on two legs, he crossed his arms over his chest and looked at her.

"And what about you, Meg? Did you have a typical childhood?"

She glanced down at the spiral notebook on the table in front of her and pulled at the loose wire on the top edge. "Well, I lived with both my parents, but I don't think you could call my childhood typical exactly."

"How come?"

She peeked up. "Because I also had a governess."

"A governess? Were you rich or something?"

Meg shrugged. "Not really, but I suppose we were fairly well-off. My parents are both professional photographers, and they work constantly. Mrs. Farnham took care of me until I went to high school. Before that, we traveled wherever my parents' assignments took them.''

''And where was that?''

She looked back down and pulled the wire out farther, twisting it around her finger. ''Oh, all over. Europe, Asia, Africa—''

The front legs of his chair landed with a thud and Meg looked up in surprise.

''You mean you've lived all over the world?'' he asked. ''You make it sound as ordinary as living in Wisconsin, Indiana and Iowa.'' Feeling like a hick, he smiled sheepishly and said, ''I guess you can tell that I'm impressed.''

Meg waved her hand and frowned. ''Don't be. It wasn't all that great.''

''How can you say that?'' he scoffed, but her sad, wistful smile convinced him that she wasn't kidding around.

''I suppose you think I was a spoiled, ungrateful child.''

''No, not at all. Please go on.'' As shy as she was, she hadn't revealed much about herself and he was anxious for her to continue.

''Well—'' She went back to fiddling with that damn wire, denying Gavin the advantage of seeing her eyes.

''Living constantly on the go as we did,'' she stated quietly, ''I never had any friends my own age to play with, which is something I've always regretted.'' She looked up, and the fragile sensitivity in her expression filled him with tenderness.

''There were times,'' she continued, ''that I couldn't even speak the language of the country we'd be in. I always felt like an outsider.''

Gavin nodded. ''I can understand that. I traveled as a child, but it wasn't so grand.''

''Really?''

Gavin could have kicked himself. Now he had to explain. And he had to be careful, or she'd have his life story right out of him.

He sighed and settled back in his chair, crossing his arms over his chest once again. "My mother was a nightclub singer, so we traveled. We lived mostly out West, though."

"Did you live in a house?"

"No, we used to rent rooms most of the time." When they weren't sleeping in their old, rusted van, he thought, but Gavin didn't think she needed to know that.

"We never owned a house, either. My parents thought a house would be a burden, and it would be with their life-style. I own my own house now, though, and I love it."

Her eyes lit up like Dennis's at Christmas and Gavin was enchanted.

"Did your aunt and uncle have a house?" she went on.

"Yes, in Kentucky. They still live there." He roused himself and crossed the room to stir the beef stew. He needed a little distance from her potent charm. She made a pretty picture, sitting there in her purple shorts outfit with her hair swept up into a ponytail. She looked fresh and attractive.

"In fact, they have a whole farm," he continued. "They raise and train horses."

"Oh, so that's where you learned so much about horses. I wondered. How come you joined the circus? Didn't you like farm life?"

Gavin's stomach tightened. The conversation was hitting a little too close to home. He put down the wooden spoon and turned, leaning against the counter.

"Farm life is okay. In fact, Dennis and I spend our winters at my aunt and uncle's. But I guess after all those years on the road, wanderlust is in my blood. What about you? If you love your house so much, how come you joined the show?"

Meg had turned in her seat, and now sat sideways. Her chin was propped on her fists on the chairback and her long, bare legs were crossed at the knee. Gavin swallowed and tried to control his heightened breathing. Resisting her had been easier when those shapely legs were under the table out of sight.

She heaved a sigh. "Joining a circus for the summer wasn't my idea, believe me." She put one wrist to her forehead and feigned a martyrlike pose. "Ah, the things we do for the sake of friendship."

Gavin grinned. "I take it that this was Carol's idea."

Meg's smile bubbled over into a tinkling laugh and she touched a finger to her nose to give him the charade sign for his having guessed correctly.

Gavin crossed his arms and raised his eyebrows. "I think you must be a pretty soft touch, Meg Harper."

Meg shook her head and stood up, gathering her pencils and notebook. "No, I was just kidding around. I mean, it was Carol's idea to join the circus for the summer. She's never had a chance to travel, you see. But I don't really mind it that much."

"Yeah, sure, and I suppose you have a bridge you think you can sell me, too."

Meg was shocked by the knowing glint in Gavin's eyes. Most people didn't understand how much she disliked traveling, but then, as she was beginning to discover, Gavin wasn't like most people.

She looked at him warily and held the spiral notebook against her chest, as if it could shield what was in her heart from his sight.

"No, I really was teasing before. Carol couldn't have talked me into it if I didn't want to come. And it is only for the summer," she stressed. "Besides, I enjoy performing in front of the circus audience."

"Whatever you say, Meg." Gavin's tone was skeptical.

"I'd better get going. I'm sure you and Dennis want to eat." And she wanted to get while the getting was good.

He walked her to the door. "All right, I'll see you later for our ride."

As he opened the trailer door, Rosa Cannone, Rico's mother, stepped up into the trailer. A large boa constrictor was draped casually around her shoulders.

"Hi, Gavin. How'd you know I was just gonna knock?"

Seeing the snake, Meg's throat tightened so she couldn't scream. Seeking safety, she slipped silently behind Gavin and held tightly to his arm.

"What the hell?" Gavin tried to turn around, but Meg clutched him until she realized her nails were cutting into his flesh.

"Gavin, don't move." She hoped he picked up the urgency in her tone. With her eyes shut tight, she almost thrust him between herself and Rosa. "I hate snakes. Keep it away from me. *Please* keep it away from me." Trying to control her irrational panic, she buried her face against the back of his shoulder, unable to look in the snake's direction. Meg knew she was acting like a fool, but she couldn't help it. She'd had this phobia ever since she was fourteen—in Egypt. A cold shiver slithered down her spine and she squeezed her eyes even tighter at the painful remembrance.

"Lucky's a pet," the woman said, her voice coming closer.

Meg shrank back against the wall, pulling Gavin with her, using him as her shield. She felt her legs go weak. "Stay away. I'm not kidding."

"I'm sorry, Rosa, but maybe you'd better go." Gavin's words were her salvation.

"Gavin, you know Lucky won't hurt her," Rosa protested.

"I know it, but she doesn't."

"Hmph. Aw right." Rosa sounded offended. Her sandals slapped against the wooden steps as she descended. "I only came over to tell you that my pa wants to leave 'bout six tomorrow mornin' for the fishin' trip."

"Great, thanks. Tell Joe that Dennis will be ready." Gavin shut the trailer door and spoke quietly. "Okay, Meg, the coast is clear. You can come out now."

She sighed, leaning against his back for support as her strength ebbed with the tension.

Gavin grabbed her left arm and turned.

She looked up guiltily. "I'm sorry."

"Shh." He wrapped his arm around her shoulders. "You're shaking like a leaf. Come sit down."

Glad of his support, she unsteadily walked to the sofa and sat. He pried her notebook and pencils from her left hand and tossed them onto an end table.

"Relax for a minute, honey. I'll be right back."

*Honey?* Meg's ears perked up at Gavin's casual use of the endearment. The warm feeling it gave her helped ease her distress as she waited for him to return from the kitchen.

Bearing a drink, Gavin entered the living room and sat down next to her. "I hope you like sherry. It's all I have that's alcoholic besides beer."

"Thanks." Meg reached for the tumbler with a shaky hand.

He sat facing her, his right booted ankle resting crosswise on his left knee. Casually clasping that ankle with his left hand, he propped his right forearm on the sofa back and leaned toward her. His nearness was overwhelming, but she had no desire to scoot farther away. On his face he wore a solicitous expression, as if he was waiting for her sign to grant him the role of comforter.

Meg's heart swelled at Gavin's offer of basic human kindness. It made no difference that she was his son's teacher, or that he traveled for a living. Any port in the storm was welcome at times like this.

Needing the security of his embrace, Meg reached out.

## Chapter Five

"Do you want to tell me what that was all about?" Gavin asked gently as he held her in his arms.

For the past several minutes, Meg had been like a sponge, soaking up strength in Gavin's reassuring embrace. She dreaded the disruption of that peaceful time, but knew Gavin deserved an explanation.

Drawing a calming breath, she sat up straight and was disappointed when Gavin removed his arm from around her shoulders and rested it on the back of the couch. She focused on the empty glass in her hands, then set it aside on the end table. "I had a bad experience with a snake when I was fourteen." She shrugged away a shiver and looked up at him. "I'm okay now."

He looked skeptical. "Right. So what was this 'bad experience' of yours?"

Unable to answer, Meg jumped up and walked over to the open window. Folding her arms across her chest, she pretended interest in the traffic on the road in the distance.

"It was nothing," she murmured.

Meg heard Gavin move behind her. She could feel his presence close by and knew he wasn't satisfied with her answer. She couldn't blame him, but she hadn't been able to speak of the incident for fourteen years. How could she now?

"Nothing, Meg?" Gavin's hands closed around her upper arms. "You wouldn't have reacted the way you did if it was nothing," he said quietly. Drawing her back against his chest, he wrapped his arms over hers. "Don't be afraid. Whatever happened can't hurt you now."

She nodded. "I know." But the memory could still scare her to death.

"Where did it happen?" he prodded gently.

With a sinking feeling, Meg realized he wasn't willing to accept her evasiveness.

"In Egypt."

"Egypt?" His tone demanded a response, and she sighed.

"Yes, my parents were there getting photos for a magazine article. Mrs. Farnham and I tagged along when they went to the temple of Kom Ombo." She turned her head, looking at him over her shoulder. "Do you remember? I told you she was my—"

"Your governess." He nodded and brought her back to the sofa. They sat side by side. "Go on," he prompted.

Knowing he wouldn't be satisfied until he had all the facts, Meg nervously glanced down at the violet appliqué on the front of her shorts and twisted a loose thread between her fingers. "We were there for several hours. My father wanted to wait for the right sun angle for one of his shots. I got bored, so I started poking around on my own."

She looked up with a smile of chagrin. "I should have known better. My parents had warned me all my life about being careful in areas like that. The threat of poisonous snakes and wild animals didn't mean much to me, though. I'd always been sheltered." She shrugged. "Besides, I was a teenager."

Gavin smiled. "You knew it all."

"I *thought* I did," she said, shaking her head in self-deprecation, "but that day I found out differently."

"Don't be too hard on yourself," he told her sympathetically. "You weren't alone. We all made mistakes as teenagers."

Meg nodded, focusing on the diamond pattern in the rug, as she recalled her teen years.

"Daydreaming was one of my favorite pastimes back then," she confided shyly. "I thought maybe I could decipher a hieroglyph no one had ever been able to solve. It would lead to something wonderful." She looked up and waved her hand dismissively. "Not like buried treasure—that would be too common. It would be more like a room full of recipes for ancient potions and medicines, miracle cures for all the illnesses known to mankind. Scientists would say it was the most important discovery of the decade."

She struck a pompous pose with her nose in the air. "Of course, I'd instantly become the most popular person in the world and everyone would want to meet me."

Gavin chuckled and she rolled her eyes, sighing at the foolishness of her girlhood fantasies. Unfortunately the remembrance of what had come after quickly sobered her. She shifted uncomfortably and folded her arms across her chest.

Gavin wrapped his arm around her shoulders. "What happened, Meg?" His tone was solicitous, but firm, and she smiled, thinking it was probably the same tone he used when training horses to do something they didn't want to do.

"It was hot that day," she explained reluctantly, seeing again the tall white columns with lotus-leaf capitals and hieroglyphic decorations. "And it was so sunny that I'd begun to get a headache from the glare. I wandered into a shady area to cool off and look around."

She shrugged. "Of course, when I first took off my sunglasses, it was hard to see. My eyes had to adjust." Knowing what had come next, Meg couldn't talk as the tension rose up to strangle her.

"Then what happened?" Gavin prompted.

She swallowed around the thickness in her throat. "I saw a movement in a corner, but it was too dim to make out what it was. The next thing I knew, something wet sprayed into my face and eyes. *It hurt so bad,*" she whispered, drawing her knees up to her chest. She huddled into a ball, the terror of the past clutching her stomach in a viselike grip. In her mind, she was there among the ruins again, chilled by the fear reaching out to her like the hand of death.

Instantly she realized what had caused the pain in her eyes. *A spitting cobra!*

Sick at the danger she was in, Meg lunged backward and spun around, forcing her shaky legs to move. Got to get away! Quick! Quick! Get out of range.

*Don't strike! Don't strike!* she frantically pleaded, sure that at any second one of her ankles would feel the piercing jab of the serpent's fangs. In the menacing silence behind her was a living, breathing threat she couldn't see.

She rubbed her eyes. The pain kept her from raising the lids.

Heat. Bright light. Meg realized she was outside now. The blood pounded so loudly in her ears she couldn't hear anything but her own harsh breathing.

"Dad-dyyy!" she screamed at the top of her lungs. "Dad-dyyy!"

She stumbled over a rock, but kept running, her arms flailing madly in the air. The pain in her eyes made her weak.

"Dad-dyyy!"

Meg suddenly became conscious that someone was holding her, talking to her. She was no longer huddled in a ball, but was wrapped in Gavin's arms. He was stroking her hair.

"It's okay, Meg. It's all over. Don't be afraid."

She hugged him, holding on tightly. Her heart was beating so fast she thought it might burst. What happened? she wondered, feeling as if she'd just awakened from a bad dream.

A few minutes later, when her heart had slowed to its normal rhythm, Meg pressed her hands to Gavin's chest and leaned back. His eyes were narrowed in concern as he gazed down at her.

"Did I scream?" she asked. Her throat felt tight as if she might have.

"No." His reply relieved her. She was afraid she'd gone bonkers.

"You looked like you wanted to, though," he added, grasping her hands and massaging them gently. "Are you okay now?" His brown eyes searched hers.

She nodded. "I think so." Turning up her lips in a wry smile, she added in false bravado, "So now you know my nightmare."

He raised his brows. "Not really. You stopped talking when something sprayed into your eyes."

"I did?"

"Yes, what was it?" His concerned frown touched her.

"Venom. From a spitting cobra. Our guide told my father that it was probably a young one because that species is usually nocturnal. It was my bad luck to be in the wrong place at the wrong time."

"Oh, God," Gavin groaned, his eyes expressing his shock. "It didn't bite you, did it?"

"No," she quickly reassured him. His appreciation of the danger she'd been in made her want to comfort him. "It ejected venom because it felt threatened. Apparently most poisonous snakes only strike as a last resort. Their poison fangs are for securing prey, not killing bumbling humans like me who take them by surprise."

Smiling crookedly, she made light of the situation as best she could. "Luckily I was blessed with a good set of lungs. My parents, Mrs. Farnham and our guide heard me screaming and came to my rescue."

"What did they do?"

"My father carried me to the van and washed my face and eyes with water. I'm not sure how he figured out what happened. I know I wasn't very coherent at the time."

She frowned. "If he hadn't acted so quickly, I could have been blinded. Instead, I merely ended up with a mild case of conjunctivitis."

"Thank God," Gavin replied so heartily that Meg had to smile.

She looked Gavin straight in the eyes. "Needless to say, that's why I'm terrified of snakes and avoid them at all costs. I'm sorry you had to witness my hysterics. I hope I didn't embarrass you in front of Rosa. I'm sure I offended her terribly."

Gavin pulled her against his side and cradled her head to his right shoulder. "Shh," he whispered. "No apologies. I wasn't embarrassed. Just worried."

Meg closed her eyes, savoring his caring and the strength of his embrace. She became aware of him as a man then, not just as another human being to cling to in a time of trouble. The attraction she felt for him rose and wouldn't be ignored. Following the urgings of her womanly instincts, Meg slipped her right arm around Gavin's waist as she relaxed against him.

To her delight, he then wrapped his left arm around her. How wonderful it would be, she thought, if his gesture was prompted by romantic feelings, rather than simple kindness.

Content for the moment in body and spirit, she kept her head on his shoulder and enjoyed the soft summer breeze that blew across them from the open window. Gavin seemed as relaxed and content as she, and Meg found the cozy snuggle very satisfying. All seemed right with the world. Her heart swelled with gratitude.

"Gavin?"

"Hmm?"

"Thanks for being so understanding. I haven't let myself think about that episode of my life since it happened. You're the first person I've ever told the whole story."

"I am?" He sounded surprised. "What about Carol?"

"Carol is my friend, but sometimes she can be a little insensitive. If I told her about it, she'd probably think it would be funny to hide a rubber snake in my bed."

"Ah, I see. In that case, I'll be sure that Dennis's toy snake is never around when you are." He kissed her forehead. The gesture made her feel very precious.

"Thanks. I'd hate to get the screaming meemies in front of him." With a sheepish smile, she looked up. "Maybe I should warn you that I also can't stand pictures of snakes."

"I'll make a note of it." Tenderness glimmered in his eyes. "You really have it bad, don't you, Meg?"

She sighed. "'Fraid so. Telling you about it just now helped, though."

"I'm glad." He seemed to hesitate, then asked, "What made you tell me?"

Only a few inches separated his compelling gaze from hers. Meg was sure Gavin would see the affection she was beginning to feel for him if they maintained the intimate eye contact, so she laid her head back against his shoulder and shrugged.

"I guess I felt I could trust you. You seem to inspire me to be a stronger person than I am. I've never had the courage to face my fear before."

Thunderstruck, Gavin couldn't reply. Meg had just paid him a great compliment. She'd given him her trust.

Trust was something he guarded as closely as his life and bestowed on only a chosen few. Trusting someone made you vulnerable. That she gave this gift to him so freely filled him with tenderness. Holding her in his arms made the temptation of responding to her sweet generosity hard to resist.

Keeping his roiling emotions in check was difficult. The urge was strong to kiss Meg, but maybe if he concentrated very hard he could hold back . . . maybe . . .

Meg wondered why Gavin didn't reply. Concerned by his silence, she slowly tilted her face up to his.

He didn't move as her gaze slowly rose from the front of the navy T-shirt stretched taut across his muscular chest upward to the crew neckline. The pulse at the base of his throat was beating as rapidly as her own. Was the same physical awareness that was affecting her affecting him?

With a pounding heart, she glanced from his Adam's apple and clean-shaven jaw to his mouth. His lips were smooth and slightly parted. A whisper of warm air tickled her eyelashes and she blinked.

Anxious to see his expression, she raised her gaze upward. Her breath caught in her throat at the desire burning in his eyes. She wouldn't look away this time. She'd wait for him to respond. If only he'd make the response she longed for....

Gavin's resistance crumbled the second Meg's wide blue gaze met his. He could see that she wanted him to kiss her. Denying himself had been difficult, but he wasn't strong enough to deny her, too.

He moved slowly, lifting his left palm to caress her cheek.

Meg thought she would burst with anticipation. Watching as Gavin slowly lowered his face to hers, she closed her eyes and strained upward to receive his kiss.

The touch of their lips lasted only a few seconds, a few *glorious* seconds, Meg thought. Hesitant, she drew back, but Gavin lifted her face and pressed his mouth more firmly against hers, coaxing her lips open at the same time.

Meg nearly jumped out of her skin at the first brush of his tongue. French-kissing had seemed sloppy and slightly repulsive on the few previous occasions she'd tried it. With Gavin, she found herself anxious for his tongue's next parry. Opening her mouth wider, she allowed him freer access and was immediately rewarded by the sensual onslaught of his tongue against hers.

Meg had never felt so alive before. Her blood raced through her veins and her nerve endings tingled wherever her body came in contact with Gavin's. Soon it seemed the hot, deep kisses weren't enough for either of them.

Gavin lifted her arms around his neck and pulled her flush against him, shifting them both into more of a reclining position as he feverishly ran his hands up and down the length of her back.

Practically lying on top of him, Meg became painfully aware of the height of his passion and quickly sobered. She turned her face, breaking off their kiss, and pushed against Gavin's chest. To her dismay, she was now pressed more fully against that part of his lower anatomy she wished to avoid. Quickly performing an awkward push-up, she barely brushed against his body as she backed away.

"Meg, where are you going?" Gavin's husky voice pulled at her resolve for constraint.

"Gavin, we've got to stop." She immediately saw reason flicker in his eyes.

He sat up, ran an unsteady hand through his hair, then gave her a sheepish grin. "Wow. I guess things got a little out of control." How could he have let one kiss escalate like that? The force of attraction he felt for Meg was obviously a lot more powerful than he'd thought. My God, the ache to make love to her was sweet torture.

Draping his arm around her shoulder, he gently tugged. "Come here. Just for a minute."

Meg was wary. "I don't know—"

He drew an invisible cross over his heart and held up his palm. "No hot and heavy stuff, I promise. I just want to hold you a little more."

Meg let him draw her into the crook of his arm.

He kissed the top of her head. "I feel a little dazed. How did all that get started, anyway?"

She looked up with a shy smile. "Well, you were comforting me because of the snake—"

"Ah, yes, Lucky." He nibbled at her lips. "I guess he really is a lucky charm."

Meg pushed him away and wrinkled her nose. "A snake?"

"That's his name," Gavin defended. "And you've got to admit that he helped bring us together." He reached up and tucked a loose strand of hair behind her ear and smiled gently. "After all that sneak-a-peek stuff at breakfast, I wasn't sure if our relationship would ever get this far."

Meg's face flamed red. "Scoundrel."

Gavin chuckled and drew her closer. Forehead to forehead, he rubbed his nose lightly against hers, then progressed into a kiss. He made sure this kiss was different than those that had gone before, keeping it soft and light. It was a kiss to melt hearts rather than enflame desires.

"Mmm. That was nice," Meg murmured afterward, and he smiled in satisfaction.

"I needed to clear up that first impression you had of me," he stated. "I had to make sure you knew that I *can* kiss without turning into a raving sex maniac."

"Oh." Meg thought about his statement, then smiled and said, "In that case, maybe I'd better make sure you know the same thing about me."

Gavin's eyes sparkled. "Sounds good."

Meg had never before initiated a kiss with a man, and she was a little intimidated. Sliding her arms around his neck, she pulled his head down to hers and poured out the tender emotion in her heart.

Gavin's moan of pleasure indicated he was enjoying her effort in his behalf, and Meg gained confidence in her feminine powers of seduction. Before Gavin, she'd been too inhibited to express her desires in a man's arms. The sense of freedom she felt now made her feel giddy and as light as a helium-filled balloon.

She was firmly entrenched in Gavin's embrace when the trailer door flew open. Startled, they broke apart.

"Hey, Dad! I'm hungry!" Dennis stopped short in the open doorway. "What are you doin'?" His eyes opened wide. "Were you two *kissin'?*" he asked loudly, a grin spreading across his gamin features.

Meg thought she'd die of embarrassment. She slid several inches away from Gavin and frantically smoothed back the hair that had fallen from her ponytail clasp.

A few people outside the trailer were attracted by Dennis's outburst. They turned to gaze in at her and Gavin.

"Shut the door!" Gavin shouted. His irritated tone revealed that he'd lost his cool, and Meg felt sorry for the boy who'd had the bad luck to walk in at the wrong time.

Dennis quickly did as his father bade, and Meg laid a restraining hand on Gavin's arm. Glancing her way, he apparently caught her message.

He sighed and looked at his son. "I'm sorry, Dennis. I shouldn't have yelled like that. Never mind what we were doing. It's time for you to set the table for dinner."

Dennis's expression lightened in the face of his father's apology. "Okay, Dad." His big brown curious eyes were riveted on them as he walked to the kitchen and Meg squirmed uncomfortably.

"I'm sorry, Meg. I had no idea he'd burst in on us like that." Gavin's chagrin touched her.

"I'll get over it." Nervously smoothing her clothes, she stood and picked up her notebook and pencils from the end table. "I'd better get going."

Gavin walked her to the door. "Hey, do me a favor, will you?"

Meg paused with her hand on the doorknob. "What?"

"Wear the ugliest thing you own to go riding later," he said quietly. "Otherwise I might not be able to keep my hands off you." The hungry look in his eyes made her pulse jump.

She grinned. "No chance." Opening the door, she hesitated and glanced outside to make sure there were no slithery creatures in sight.

Gavin's voice rumbled close to her ear. "Want me to check for you?"

Touched, Meg shook her head. "No, I'll check. If I ever hope to get over this thing, I'll have to start getting tough with myself. And, as they say, there's no time like the present." She kissed him on the cheek. "But thanks for the offer."

Gavin watched from the doorway as Meg marched forward, head held high, and he envied her her courage. She had plenty of insecurities, but she also had an internal fortitude he was ashamed to admit he was lacking. One more reason he shouldn't get involved with her, he thought. This reason was for her own good, rather than his. She deserved better. Turning away, he closed the door.

Later that afternoon, Meg smiled as she applied liniment before donning her blue jeans and multicolored circus T-shirt. Not even the obnoxious odor could squelch her happiness and good temper.

Looking forward to her ride with Gavin, she sauntered into the horse tent with an air of expectancy. Just seeing his back as he saddled Ginger made her pulse race. The navy fabric stretched taut across his broad shoulders reminded her of the strength of his embrace, and Meg drew in a deep breath at the curling sensation in her stomach.

"Hi." She stopped next to him with a huge smile plastered on her face.

He glanced up briefly, and the wary look in his eyes puzzled her. "Hi. I'm just about done here. You can go ahead and mount Misty." He looked back down at the strap he was tightening.

"By myself?"

He avoided her gaze. "I think you can manage it after all the practice you had yesterday. Don't forget to put on your hat first."

"Okay." Disappointed that he wasn't going to take advantage of an opportunity to, as he'd said, "get his hands on her," she slipped on the hard hat he'd given her the day before. Patting Misty on the neck in greeting, she untied the reins and held them in her left hand, then grabbed the saddle horn and raised her left foot to the stirrup.

"Ugh." Her sore muscles protested, but she managed to pull herself up into the saddle unassisted. She smiled down at Gavin to share the joy of her accomplishment, but he was gathering his own reins, preparing to mount and didn't notice. The smile died on her lips, and Meg wondered what had happened to the man who'd paid her so much warm attention only a short while earlier.

He mounted and turned. "All set?"

Meg nodded, disappointed by his seeming indifference.

They rode in silence out to the nearby abandoned cow pasture of a Wisconsin farm that was being redeveloped. Meg let Gavin ride a little ahead of her while she concentrated on concealing her hurt feelings.

He stopped, waiting for her to catch up. "Too bad about all this farmland," he commented as she drew near. "Looks like it's being developed for housing from the way the stakes are laid out."

She glanced around, unable to work up much enthusiasm. "At least it's not going to be a strip shopping center."

He nodded, his gaze narrowed on the farmland in the distance. "Unfortunately it'll only be a matter of time before they spring up around here, too."

Proud of the way she'd kept her tone neutral, Meg managed to ask, "Well, what's on the agenda for today?"

"Trotting."

"Trotting," she parroted, and wrinkled her nose. "That's the bouncy gait, isn't it?"

A slow grin spread across his face and his eyes sparkled as he drawled, "Yep." His expression warmed her.

"Oh, great. As if my body doesn't ache enough already," she groused, smiling to let him know her complaint was good-natured.

He shrugged. "So use the liniment." The soft light in his eyes betrayed the fact that he wasn't as unsympathetic as he sounded, and Meg took heart. For whatever reason he was playing hard to get, he wasn't completely insensitive to her.

"I've got it on now, as you can very well tell," she admonished.

"You mean, as I can very well *smell*."

"*As the whole county can very well smell*," she announced, gesturing her arm in a wide arc. They shared a smile, and Meg was pleased that Gavin had lost his wary look. He didn't treat her with the same intimacy he'd displayed earlier that day, but his teasing was a step in the right direction.

Distressed by his change in attitude, Meg's insecurities came rolling back. Had she mistaken his kisses for more than just physical attraction? Her fragile self-confidence cracked and she couldn't bring herself to ask him what was wrong. If he wanted to deny what happened between them earlier, Meg decided she would, too. She had her pride, after all, and was determined not to let him see how unhappy she was. She'd concentrate on her riding lesson.

"Try it again, Meg." Gavin's patience was wearing thin. For the past half hour, he'd been trying to teach Meg to trot properly, but the lesson was not going well. She couldn't seem to get the hang of the horse's rhythm. He could tell she was getting frustrated and knew it was his fault for holding back. He felt like a heel for treating her so callously, but knew it was for the best. Things had gotten out of hand earlier. He was determined to cool it for a while.

With another failed attempt, Meg stopped her horse in front of him. "I'm beginning to feel like a human basketball, a very deflated human basketball," she said wearily.

Gavin's heart ached to see her looking so defeated. "Why don't we give it up for today? You should rest before the show."

Meg lifted her hat and wiped a trickle of sweat off her forehead, then replaced the hat on her head. "Could we ride around this pasture first? I hate to go back without accomplishing something positive."

"Sure."

They walked their horses side by side around the perimeter of the field. The hot wind and swirling dust were almost as suffocating as the heavy silence between them, but Gavin saw the dark clouds piling up to the west. He was just about to comment on the coming rain when Meg spoke up.

"Did Dennis have anything else to say about what happened this afternoon?" Her voice cracked on the last word and Gavin realized it had cost her a lot to bring up the subject.

"Yeah." He swallowed hard in remembrance of his son's question. "He wanted to know if we were going to get married."

"Married?" She pulled back on Misty's reins, halting, as her round-eyed gaze displayed the same shock he'd felt when he'd heard the question. It was comforting to know she was as rattled by the thought as he'd been.

"Don't worry," he assured her. "I straightened him out." Turning in his saddle, he said, "Come on. We haven't got time to stop. Rain's on the way."

Meg caught up. "Does Dennis ask that about all the women you kiss?"

He grunted. "Dennis has never seen me kiss a woman before, so he jumped to conclusions."

"Never?" Her tone of voice told him she didn't believe him, and he frowned.

"I told you before that I don't have time for that sort of thing."

"You had time this afternoon. Surely you must have had other opportunities—"

"Listen, Meg." He stopped and she halted beside him. Gavin looked at her sharply, ready to tell her to mind her own business, but the sadness clouding her blue eyes pierced his heart. The biting remark he'd been about to make died before it reached his lips. He sighed, defeated by her vulnerability.

Gently he explained. "My wife left me before Dennis was a year old. We were divorced when he was two. I was angry and bitter and wanted nothing to do with women for a long time."

"For four years?"

"No, not that long." He slanted her a wry grin.

"But you said you haven't kissed—" Her confusion was obvious, and Gavin interrupted.

"I don't think you understand. I said that I haven't kissed anyone *in front of* Dennis. That doesn't mean that I haven't had relationships with women."

"Oh." Meg's expression was thoughtful, and Gavin hoped that would end the subject.

A strong gust of wind brought the heavy scent of rain, and narrowing his eyes, Gavin turned and studied the brewing storm. Lightning split the dark sky in the distance and was followed by the low rumble of thunder.

"Let's go." He led the way, then called over his shoulder, "Do you think you can pick up the pace? We'll never get back before the storm hits if we don't."

"I'll try." Meg wasn't thrilled about the idea of getting caught in a thunderstorm, especially on horseback. What were a few more bone-jarring minutes, anyway? Following Gavin's example, she squeezed her legs, and Misty broke into a trot. She concentrated on moving with the rhythm of the horse.

"Hey, Meg!"

She looked up to see Gavin's smile. "What?"

"You're doing it!"

"I'm doing what?" she asked, then raised her eyebrows. "Trotting the right way?"

"Yep. How does it feel?" The warm approval in Gavin's eyes made her glow.

"It feels great!"

They reached the perimeter of the circus grounds just as large, fat raindrops began to fall. An eerie chorus of animal sounds rose above the howl of the wind as roustabouts and show people scurried around tying down side ropes and whatever could blow away in the wind.

Gavin and Meg quickly dismounted at the horse tent. Two of the cowboys in the show volunteered to take care of their mounts for them.

"Thanks, guys." Gavin handed over the reins, then turned to Meg. "You'd better get over to clown alley and see what needs to be done." He tilted his head to one side. "I've got plenty to keep me busy until show time. You did good today," he added.

She smiled lopsidedly. "Yeah, sure, once the storm got my mind off what I was doing. Tomorrow I'll probably forget how I did it."

He shook his head. "You can do anything you put your mind to." His compelling eyes lit with a heartrending tenderness, and, for a moment, she thought he might kiss her. Instead, he chucked her under the chin. "I have to go. See you later."

She followed him out into the driving rain, where he began checking the side ropes on the horse tent. Meg spared him one last glance. She'd been dismissed for now, but she had a date with him the next day. Maybe then she could figure out why he'd closed her out. Or better yet, maybe he would open up...

## Chapter Six

The next morning, Meg and Carol had already finished breakfast when Gavin arrived at the cook tent for his meal. Meg had been watching for him and her pulse leaped when she finally saw his tall form duck around the canvas opening.

He paused just inside and slid back the hood of his yellow rain slicker, revealing his wet, neatly combed hair. His gaze skimmed across the crowd until he found her watching him. The gloom of the rainy day was chased away by his instant smile.

Meg waited expectantly as he carried his tray directly toward the table where she was seated with Carol and two of the Alexander brothers, the unmarried ones. She saw Gavin hesitate when he noticed with whom she was sitting, but she waved him over.

"Hi, everybody," he said, setting down his tray next to Meg and shedding his slicker.

Returning his greeting along with everyone else, Meg scooted over toward Kurt Alexander, allowing Gavin more room to fold his long legs through the opening of the picnic-style table. She was startled by the feel of a hand caressing her jean-covered thigh, Kurt Alexander's hand. Hoping no one noticed, she lifted Kurt's hand and set it back on his own leg.

Gavin's raised eyebrow and sidelong glance indicated he'd caught the furtive movement and questioned what was going on, but Meg just smiled in embarrassed silence, then scooted back toward Gavin once he was seated.

From across the table, Carol picked up the conversation where it had left off and asked, "So what does everyone do around here on their day off?"

"Oh, various things," Ivan replied, next to Carol. "Some practice or work on new material, others do their laundry, or sleep." He shrugged. "Whatever they feel like."

"Ivan and I explore," Kurt offered. "You know, like check out what's happening around town. You two interested in coming along?"

"Sure," Carol piped up.

Meg felt Gavin tense beside her and quickly said, "No, thanks, I have other plans." She hadn't yet told Carol about her date with Gavin and now regretted not mentioning it.

"What plans?" Carol asked with her typical bluntness.

"Just plans," Meg said firmly, staring directly into her friend's eyes. She didn't want to say anything that would put Gavin on the spot. Since he hadn't told her when or where they were going, she was afraid he'd forgotten he'd asked her to spend the day with him, or worse yet, changed his mind. He'd acted so distant during their ride yesterday that she didn't know what to think.

With a puzzled frown, Carol glanced from Meg to Gavin, then back again. Meg smiled and the spark of understanding glimmered in Carol's eyes. "Oh, okay."

"Carol, you'll still come, won't you?" asked Ivan.

"Sure."

"We'll give you a rain check, Meg," Kurt added, "for when you don't have plans." He stood up. "Let's hit the road."

Ivan and Carol rose to follow Kurt.

Carol winked at Meg. "Bye. Have fun today."

"You, too." She smiled, but a worried frown knit her brows as she watched her friend go off with the Alexander brothers. Something about the two made her uneasy.

She turned to Gavin, who was eating his cereal, and asked, "Do you know Kurt and Ivan very well?"

His spoon paused halfway to his lips. "No."

Seeing Ivan's arm slide around Carol's shoulders, Meg pursed her lips and frowned deeper. "Do you know them at all?"

Gavin ate his bite of cereal, then laid down his spoon very deliberately. "Some. This is their second season with the show."

"What do you know about them?" Seeing his scowl, she added, "If you don't mind my asking."

"Actually I do mind," he said curtly. "If you wanted to get to know them better, why didn't you go with them?"

Meg opened her mouth in surprise. "I didn't want to go with them."

"Oh, really?" Gavin's voice was heavy with sarcasm. "Is that why you looked so unhappy when they left without you?"

"I'm not unhappy—"

"Meg," Gavin's sharp tone made heads turn, and he dropped his voice. "Let's cut to the chase," he said quietly. "If you want to go out with Kurt, fine. Just be straight with me."

Meg couldn't believe her ears. Gavin had misconstrued her reason for asking about the brothers and had the nerve to act as if she'd just done something wrong.

Irritated, she glanced from his empty tray to his waiting expression. "If you're done eating, I'd like to discuss this someplace else."

"Fine." He stood up and they gathered their belongings.

Meg thrust her arms into the sleeves of her blue cotton jacket and turned up the collar.

"Is that all you've got? Don't you have a raincoat?" Gavin asked, slipping into his slicker. The criticism in his tone added fuel to her growing irritation.

She turned her back on him and strode out of the tent, then stopped suddenly when she realized she didn't know where to go. Turning around, she squinted at him in the pouring rain. "Where do you want to talk?"

"How about my trailer?"

"No."

"How come? Dennis isn't there. It'll be private."

Too private, she thought. Besides, if she took one look at the sofa where he'd kissed her so thoroughly the day before, she'd lose all her steam. Right now she was too aggravated to let that happen.

"It's not neutral territory," she finally answered, hunching her shoulders against the cool water that trickled down her neck.

"Well, where do you want to talk?" he asked in a tone of exaggerated patience.

Tight-lipped, she glanced around. "The horse tent."

"Fine."

Meg slipped and slid precariously over the gooey ground. Now she knew why traveling circuses were sometimes referred to as mud shows. With each step her sneakers seemed to sink deeper and deeper into the mire. Gavin, she noticed grumpily, was having no trouble walking in his rubber boots. What was worse, his slicker covered so much of him that not even his face got wet. Knowing he was right about her not being adequately dressed for the weather did nothing to improve her mood.

Hearing his exasperated sigh, she looked up.

He grasped her upper arm to help her negotiate the slippery ground, but his expression was so disapproving that Meg didn't feel grateful.

Once inside the horse tent, she jerked her arm from his grasp. "What's your problem, Gavin?"

Several horses turned their heads and raised their ears, nickering at the disturbance, but Meg paid them little mind.

Her quick glance around the tent assured her they'd have privacy, something normally hard to come by on the circus grounds. At least the rain was good for something.

Gavin took his time answering, pausing first to shrug off his slicker and toss it over a stool. When he turned back, his expression was no longer antagonistic. His gaze searched hers.

"Meg, why didn't you tell Kurt you had a date with me today?" he asked quietly. The glimmer of hurt she saw in his brown eyes, the hurt he was trying to conceal behind his scowl, evaporated her anger.

"That's why— Oh, Gavin. I'm sorry. I didn't mean to hurt your feelings."

"Don't worry about it," he blustered. "Just answer my question."

She frowned in reproach, then sighed, acknowledging that her irritation with him stemmed partly from her own hurt feelings.

"Frankly I wasn't sure if we were still on for today," she admitted. "I didn't want to be presumptuous in case you'd changed your mind."

"Why would you think I'd done that?"

She shrugged, and glanced down, unable to meet his gaze. "Yesterday afternoon you seemed . . . distant."

When he didn't answer, she turned and watched the rain pour down outside the tent. His silence filled her with a sad emptiness. Why was he shutting her out?

Chilled by the cool, wet fabric of her jacket clinging to her arms, she shivered. Though the horse-scented air inside the tent was quite warm, goose bumps rose on her flesh.

"Are you cold?" Gavin asked, concern apparent in his voice. "Your jacket is soaked. You'd better take it off." He walked up behind her, peeled the jacket off and tossed it on a bale of hay then ran his hands up and down her bare arms. His palms were warm and slightly rough, his touch gentle and tender. Meg fought the awareness that filled her. How did this man manipulate her pulse so easily?

When she turned, his expression was thoughtful.

"Meg, I'm sorry I acted so—uh, that is, if you're interested in going out with Kurt, that's your business. I had no right to give you such a difficult time about it." He dropped his hands from her arms, but Meg grasped his hands in hers before he could step away.

She looked up into his eyes. "Gavin, I'm not interested in Kurt."

"No?" His tone said he didn't quite believe her.

She shook her head. "At least, not in the way you think. I'm just worried about Carol going off with the two of them. You saw how forward Kurt was with me at breakfast." Her face grew warm as she realized how prim she sounded. She wished she could retract her last statement.

Gavin quirked an eyebrow. "Do you mean because he held your hand under the table?"

"He didn't hold my hand," she denied. "He grabbed my thigh in a way—" She paused. "Well, let's just say that I don't appreciate such familiarity from a stranger," she said heatedly. "What you saw was me putting his hand back into his own lap where it belonged."

"Oh, that's all that was." Gavin smiled, as if relieved, and Meg hit him on the arm.

"Hey! What was that for?" he asked, grabbing his arm.

"How dare you think I'm the kind of woman who goes around kissing one man one day and then holding hands with another the next!" Trying not to smile at his indignant expression as he rubbed the spot where she'd hit him, Meg was about to give him a second playful punch for good measure, but Gavin grabbed her fist and pinned both her arms behind her.

"Hold on there, slugger. You made your point. I apologize for the error."

Held tight against Gavin's chest, Meg looked up. His eyes reflected the same electric shock she felt, and she noticed his breathing accelerate.

Suspended in time with their gazes locked, Meg and Gavin didn't move. The heart-stopping moment was filled with sweet possibilities, hidden desires only guessed at, and longings neither was ready to put into words.

Gavin looked away, and the intimate spell was broken.

Meg squeezed her eyes shut and inhaled unsteadily, her disappointment warring with a sense of relief.

He let go of her arms and stepped back. "Well..." He cleared his throat. "You needn't worry about Carol. I know Kurt and Ivan well enough to know they won't harm her."

"Good," she murmured, unable to reconcile herself with the loss of his touch.

"That's not to say one of them won't try something," he added. "They've earned their good-time-Charlie reputations."

"So I gathered." Meg smiled dryly. "I guess I won't worry as long as you say they're okay. I trust your judgment."

Gavin hesitated, then looked pleased. He bent and picked up her wet jacket from the hay where he'd dropped it. Squeezing out the excess water, he looked up and asked, "Will you trust my judgment on one more thing?"

"What?"

"Take my advice and buy yourself a decent raincoat and pair of boots. You'll be much more comfortable."

She took her jacket from his hands. "I'd planned on doing just that. With all the hot, dry weather we've been having, the need for rain gear slipped my mind."

"Then we'd better take you shopping first thing," he said, reaching up to smooth back a wet strand of her hair from her cheek. "We can go to the mall down the road. I need to pick up a birthday gift for my Aunt May, too."

"Okay." Meg took a deep breath as his gentle touch threatened to disrupt her equilibrium. "I'll need my purse. It's back at the camper."

He held his rain slicker over both their heads, and she raised her brows in surprise.

"Your jacket's too wet to do any good," he explained. "You can share mine."

"Thanks," she whispered, pleased by his consideration.

Each holding one end of the slicker over their heads, they dashed to Meg's camper. As if the clouds had been waiting for them to come out from under cover, the sky opened up and the rain drenched them.

Squinting her eyes against the drops pelting her face, Meg fumbled at the lock and finally opened the camper door.

Diving in behind her, Gavin held his arms and wet slicker away from his body and howled, "Look at me, woman! This is all your fault! I should have left you to your own devices."

Laughing at their equally sodden shirts, jeans and dripping hair, she shook her head. "Tsk. Tsk. Gallantry, Warner. Remember gallantry."

She stepped away to get a towel and suddenly felt herself hauled backward by a strong arm around her middle. Surprised, she turned and found herself staring into a pair of dark eyes glittering with desire.

"Gallantry be damned," came Gavin's husky reply. His kiss was swift and sure, arching her backward in its intensity.

Meg wrapped her arms around his neck to keep from falling over. Liquid heat rushed through her veins as she clung to him and opened her mouth to his searing possession. The kiss was hot and steamy and so was Meg's reaction to it. Fire licked at her nerve endings wherever her body touched his and desire throbbed deep within her.

Gavin broke off the kiss, but continued to hold her tightly against him.

"Damn," he swore softly, as if angry at himself, then said, "I'm no saint, Meg. Get out of that wet T-shirt and into something dry. I'll be back for you when the rain lets up."

He turned and dashed away into the rain as if the hounds of hell were after him.

Puzzled, and still suffering quivery aftereffects from his kiss, Meg closed the door. She walked to the bathroom for a towel and the mirror over the sink showed her what Gavin must have seen. She gasped. The wet, white fabric of her shirt clung to her breasts like a second skin, its transparency clearly delineating the lacy fabric of her bra.

Embarrassed, Meg stripped off her saturated clothing and dried herself, wondering why fate had conspired against her. This was the second time Gavin had caught her in a wet T-shirt. Had his motivation for kissing her been purely physical? she wondered disappointedly. How much nicer it would have been if his kiss had been the result of the camaraderie of getting caught in the rain together.

As attracted as she was to the sexy Gavin Warner, Meg was determined not to let lust get in the way of their relationship. She dressed in a fresh pair of jeans, then donned a red tank top, and a colorful overblouse patterned in huge tropical flowers. No matter how wet she might get, nothing would show beneath so many opaque layers.

A half hour passed before the rain let up, allowing Meg plenty of time to compose herself. She dried her wavy shoulder-length chestnut hair and fixed her makeup, then added a dash of perfume.

When a knock sounded at her door, she quickly pulled it open. Her eyes devoured the handsome figure in dry blue jeans and a yellow knit shirt, and she knew her resolution was in danger of going right out the window. She nervously twisted her purse's ropelike handle in her tight fists.

"All set?" he asked brightly, as if their earth-shattering kiss had never taken place. The man was as changeable as the tide.

"All set." Locking the camper door, Meg chastised herself for letting Gavin get to her. The way he ran hot and cold kept throwing her off balance. She knew she'd better get her guard up before she got hurt.

Gavin sniffed the light, flowery cloud of scent surrounding Meg and swallowed hard. Determined to hold his natural inclinations in check, he stepped back to keep from taking her arm. He wasn't willing to tempt his willpower by touching her. His strong physical attraction to a woman had deceived him once before. He'd learned the hard way how quickly a relationship could fall apart when good sex was all that bound two people together. His hasty marriage to Lydia had been a disaster.

They'd both been young and had fallen in love at first sight. If they had taken the time to get to know each other before rushing into marriage, they'd both have been better off. The fact that Lydia hadn't thought less of him when Gavin had confessed his illiteracy to her before he'd proposed had made him think she was the perfect woman for him. Unfortunately he had soon learned differently.

Gavin still couldn't understand how she could have been more concerned about losing her figure than bearing a child, *his* child. Other circus women he knew had had babies and then regained their figures. He'd forgiven Lydia's negative reaction to pregnancy, but he hadn't been able to forgive her rejection of Dennis, or her rejection of *him*.

Inhaling a calming breath, Gavin forced himself to relax. He was older and wiser now. He wasn't going to confuse lust with love. Besides, he had Dennis to think of. Meg was teaching Dennis to read, and he didn't want any romantic entanglements messing that up. For his son's sake, as well as his own, he knew he had to resist his attraction to Meg.

He led the way to his pickup, which he'd unhitched from his trailer, and drove them to the nearby mall. Their occasional spurts of small talk were all that broke the strained silence. Relieved when they finally entered the enclosed shopping center, Gavin hoped the distraction of the stores and the noisy hubbub of milling bodies would ease the tension. Unfortunately neither of them seemed able to relax.

Gavin followed Meg through two department stores and a sporting goods store before she found the rain gear she wanted. With her purchase of a bright yellow slicker and matching yellow rubber boots completed, he suggested they slow down to a more leisurely pace.

"You really shop with a vengeance, don't you?" he teased as they walked back out into the mall proper. "I've never seen anybody move through a store as fast as you do."

She blushed. "I'm sorry. Did you see something you wanted?"

"No, I just thought women liked to window-shop. You never even looked in a window."

"Habit," she declared. "I tend to spend less money that way."

"Well, I'm a browser. Do you mind if we just walk around for a while?"

"No, I don't mind."

"Good. I have no idea what to get my aunt. Maybe you could help me out with a few suggestions. But first—" He took her elbow in a strictly platonic manner and steered her to a small shop. "The smell of baking cookies has been driving me crazy. I don't know about you, but I've got to have one."

She smiled wryly. "Oh, great. And here I'd just convinced myself that I could survive without succumbing to the temptation." Her resistance was halfhearted and the devil in him rose to the occasion.

"No one can resist chocolate chip cookies right out of the oven." He led them to the end of the line and inhaled. "Just imagine," he said quietly, bending close to her ear, "you can almost taste the sweet, melty chocolate. And the dough, mmm. So warm and soft and chewy."

"All right, all right, I give in. You've got me drooling." She frowned up at him, but the sparkle in her eyes gave away her true feelings. "That wasn't very nice."

He grinned. "I know, but it was fun."

Meg's short burst of laughter was like a pressure valve releasing the tension inside both of them. She hadn't appeared to be having a very good time with him earlier, but now things looked more promising.

Gavin bought a small bag of freshly baked chocolate chip cookies and offered her one. He happily watched as she bit into the cookie, but then his heart stopped. The smile of sensual satisfaction that spread over her features as she closed her eyes and tilted back her head sparked all sorts of longings—longings he'd already decided were off limits. Gritting his teeth, he forced himself to look at the ugly red metal sculpture standing in the center of the mall.

"Aren't you having a cookie?" she asked, her tone surprised.

"Huh? Oh, yeah." Startled, he quickly shoved one into his mouth, barely tasting it. Thank God they were in a public place, he thought. Otherwise he would have been inclined to do other things that would have drawn the same look of sensual satisfaction from her. God, all he could think about was kissing her again. He had to get control of himself.

"So what types of things does your aunt like?" Meg asked, strolling on beyond the cookie shop.

Gavin fell into step beside her, trying to retrieve his scattered thoughts. "Oh, it's hard to say."

She wrinkled her nose at him. "That's not very helpful. Does she like perfume? Jewelry? Books?"

"Not really." He scowled, focusing his attention on the challenge of thinking of something to buy his aunt. "She likes unusual things. Maybe we should just browse around. I'll know it when I see it."

They wandered in and out of stores for more than an hour, and Gavin still hadn't found the something special he was looking for. Afraid that Meg was beginning to grow bored, he raised no objection when she decided to stop at a bookstore.

"Go right ahead," he said. "I can meet you back here later."

"No, I need your opinion on something. It'll only take a few minutes." She strode into the bookstore, obviously expecting him to follow, and Gavin inhaled deeply to control his rising panic.

Hesitating on the threshold, he quickly weighed his options. If he entered, he knew he'd have a hard time faking his ability to read if she asked him about a book. But if he didn't enter, Meg was sure to ask why.

With no real choice, he nervously walked into the bookstore, a feeling of dread pressing down on his chest. Swallowing around the tightness in his throat, he focused on the back of Meg's head and followed her down the center aisle.

The surrounding shelves seemed to close in around him, but he refused to be intimidated. He'd gotten through tight situations like this before. He just had to rely on his wits.

She ducked down a side aisle and stopped. Gavin could tell by the pictures on the bookcovers that they were in the children's area.

"I thought I'd pick up a few books for Dennis," she explained, searching the shelves. "He's ready for easy readers."

"What about the books he has at home?" Gavin asked, wondering if he'd blundered as soon as the words left his mouth.

"Most of them are too difficult for him right now," she answered without looking up. She pulled two books off the shelf and handed them to him. "What do you think about these? Do you think he'd like them?"

Gavin stared down at the two thin paperback books in his hands, then turned them over, pretending to read the printing on the back cover. Casually he flipped the books back over to concentrate on the pictures on the covers. One was of a dinosaur and the other was of a robot. Fairly confident that that's what the books were about, he answered, "Sure, he'd probably like these."

Meg stooped to scour the lower shelves, and Gavin took advantage of the opportunity to mop his brow and upper lip. She looked up just as he was stuffing his handkerchief into his pants pocket.

"Are you okay?" she asked, handing him three other books to look over as she took back the first two.

"Yeah, but it's a little stuffy in here, don't you think?"

She stood up and shrugged. "A little." Pointing to the book with a famous cartoon character on the cover, she said, "This story's cute. Most of my first-graders like it. Or do you think he'd prefer the cowboy book?"

"No, not the cowboy book," Gavin said, handing it back to her. "Dennis spends enough time being a cowboy in the show. I think he'd be bored reading about something he can already do."

"Good point." Meg replaced the book on the shelf.

The final book had a nondescript cover and Gavin almost choked. Now what? Feeling his face heat up, he quickly shrugged and handed the books back to Meg. "You decide about the rest. You're the teacher." He glanced around at the rest of the store, pretending an interest and hoping she'd hurry and make up her mind.

Meg fanned out the four books in her hands. To Gavin's relief, she slid the one with the nondescript cover back on the shelf.

"I think I'll get him these three," she stated, picking up her shopping bag.

Gavin followed her up to the checkout counter, relieved to be off the hook. When she started pulling out her wallet to pay, he put his hand out to stop her.

"I'll pay for the books."

"No, that's okay. This was my idea—"

"Meg, you're already teaching Dennis. The least I can do is pay for his books."

Recognizing the stubborn edge to his tone, Meg backed down. "Okay, suit yourself." She wasn't about to start an argument over the purchase of a few small books. If Gavin felt the need to buy them for his son, fine. She just hoped he'd spend time reading them with Dennis. She was a little disappointed he hadn't shown more interest in the books' selection.

They continued to stroll leisurely through the mall in search of a gift for Gavin's aunt. Weaving in and out of the small shops that lined the aisles, Meg learned a lot about his personal likes and dislikes.

His taste in music was similar to hers. They both liked sixties rock 'n' roll, easy listening, some classical and some country and western. His favorite foods were Italian—pasta, pizza, meatballs, sausage. She could identify with that. His taste in clothing was conservative. When he wasn't in the show, he lived mostly in blue jeans and knit shirts, anything he didn't have to iron. She could identify with that, too.

What surprised her was that he was very particular about the gift he chose for his aunt. He wasn't content to buy the first thing that caught his eye. He put a lot of time and thought into selecting the perfect birthday present. His aunt was obviously very special to him.

His eyes lit up and a satisfied smile spread across his face as they were walking through a kitchen-goods store. Turning her way, he said, "I found it."

Curious, Meg followed his gaze to a large soup tureen. The cream-colored crockery had an old-fashioned country charm about it with its relief pattern of hand-painted vegetables on two sides. The style would lend itself to a homey kitchen table, rather than a formal dining room, and Meg got an insight into the type of woman Aunt May was.

Gavin lifted the tureen carefully to examine it. "Except during the summer, Saturday night is soup night at my aunt and uncle's," he confided. "Aunt May bakes bread to go with it, too." His features softened in remembrance. "Man, you think you've died and gone to heaven when you walk into the house at suppertime. There's nothing like the smell of fresh-baked bread and home-cooked soup."

Meg smiled, thoroughly charmed by the homey image he conjured up. "That does sound like heaven."

Gavin set down the tureen. "That's nice of you to say, but you don't have to pretend that bread and soup sound that wonderful. If you've lived all over the world, you must have enjoyed all sorts of great, exotic food that I've never even heard of."

"Nope."

Gavin hesitated, as if unsure that she was being truthful. "You haven't?"

"No." She fluttered her hand. "I should qualify that. I was served lots of things you'd probably find unusual, but I can't say I enjoyed them. Give me a cheeseburger any day."

He grinned. "Really?"

"Yes, really." She shook her head and admonished, "You shouldn't go around making rash assumptions about people. Eating homemade bread and soup in a cozy kitchen would have been a real treat. When I was growing up, I either ate in the large dining room of wherever we were staying, or my parents hired cooks to make our meals and then serve them to us in our rooms." She gave him a wry look. "My parents didn't have time to include food preparation in their hectic life-style."

"What about your governess?"

"Oh, no." Meg shook her head vehemently. "Mrs. Farnham *hated* to cook." She ran her fingers over the raised vegetable pattern on the tureen. "So are you going to get this for your aunt?"

"Yes." Gavin toted the heavy tureen up to the cashier and set it down, then turned her way as they waited for the woman to finish with the customer ahead of them. "So if your mother and governess didn't teach you how to cook, who did?" he asked.

"My home economics teacher in high school." Meg leaned her elbow on the wooden counter and chuckled. "She couldn't believe how inept I was."

Gavin raised one eyebrow, the gesture Meg had come to learn meant he thought someone was putting him on.

"No fooling," she assured him. "I shouldn't admit this, because you'll probably think I'm really dumb, but that old joke about not being able to boil water applies to me."

He made a skeptical face. "Come on."

"At least, it used to apply to me," she corrected.

"I find that hard to believe, Meg. You're too smart—"

She held up her hand and laughed at his stubborn refusal to believe her. Knowing he thought that highly of her gave her a warm feeing, but she wanted him to like her for whom she was, not whom he thought she was.

"I can see I'm going to have to prove it to you." She shook her head. "Lesson one. Egg cookery. My job was to hard-boil three eggs. I got out a small saucepan, half filled it with water, then turned on the gas stove.''

Gavin nodded. ''And?''

''When the water started to boil, I carefully placed the eggs in the pot, as I'd been instructed, then set the timer for fifteen minutes.''

He frowned. ''Yeah. So?''

''Well, after I read the lesson about the other types of egg cookery that the rest of the girls in the class were doing, I got bored. I decided to do my Algebra homework while I waited for the timer to go off.'' She grimaced.

''What happened?'' he asked, his tone cautious.

''The eggs exploded.''

''Huh?''

She shrugged innocently. ''No one told me the flame wasn't supposed to lick up the sides of the pot. I figured that if you were going to boil something, you had to have a big flame.''

''So the water evaporated before the timer went off,'' he concluded, the corners of his mouth quivering with the smile she could tell he was trying to hold back.

She nodded and wrinkled her nose. ''What a stink! Poor Miss Lindstrom is probably still scraping egg off the ceiling.''

Gavin's laugh rolled from his chest in rich, baritone notes catching the attention of all the women in the store. Meg saw their expressions gleam with interest. She felt proud that she was the one with Gavin, but then stopped short when she realized what she was doing.

Since when did she start getting proprietorial? Meg asked herself. This new emotion he'd generated inside her definitely wasn't healthy. She had no claim on Gavin. She'd be crazy to allow herself to fantasize that she ever could have. It was one thing to enjoy his company and share a few romantic kisses with him, but it was quite another to start thinking of him in a possessive manner.

No, she wouldn't even consider the possibility that she could feel seriously about him. She'd be leaving the circus at the end of the summer and going back to her own house and her regular job. Meg's life was settled and she was content with it. When she got back to Rockford, she could even try making her own homemade soup and baked bread. She could achieve her dreams without Gavin. Right? Right. She hoped.

"Can I help you?" The saleswoman's question interrupted her thoughts.

"I'd like this," Gavin told her. "And please box it very carefully. I don't want it to break."

"Yes, sir." The matronly saleswoman smiled benevolently from him to Meg. "Aren't you the lucky one? I wish my husband would buy me something as nice as this."

"Oh, it's not for me," Meg quickly assured her, shocked that the woman thought she and Gavin were married. Glancing sideways, she saw that he was grinning. What was so funny? she wondered, not very pleased by his reaction.

"It's for my aunt," he explained to the woman. "I'd like you to ship it out of state."

The saleswoman looked embarrassed. "Sorry." She gave Meg a sympathetic look that seemed to add that she was sorry the gift wasn't for Meg.

Meg glanced away. Her eyes had to be playing tricks on her. Or else the sweet smell of burning incense from the gift shop next door was making her imagine things. She ignored the pang of sadness triggered by the woman's supposed sympathy.

The saleslady reached under the counter and handed Gavin a ballpoint pen and a form. "You'll have to fill this out, sir. The shipping insurance is extra. The rates are at the bottom. If you'll excuse me, I'll take this to the back and box it up." She turned to a young woman, who was stocking shelves. "Joanie, can you take over here till I get back?"

"No problem." The young woman named Joanie walked over to the abandoned wooden counter and greeted the elderly couple who were next in line. "Can I help you?"

Meg glanced back at Gavin, who was frowning down at the form.

He looked up and gave her a sheepish grin. "Can I ask a favor of you?"

"What is it?" Did he need to borrow money? she wondered. The tureen was rather expensive.

"Could you fill this out for me? I...I don't have my contacts in." His red face indicated how embarrassed he was, and Meg took pity on him.

"Sure. Hand it over."

He gave her the form and pen. "Thanks."

"I didn't realize you wore contacts," she said, studying his eyes. Had they ever looked different?

"I don't very often," he mumbled.

She nodded. "I'm not surprised with all the dust that flies around the show. Do you have the hard or soft kind?"

"Uh...hard." His eyes shifted to the doorway where the saleswoman had disappeared with the tureen. "Maybe we should get on with the form before she gets back."

Meg didn't understand why he was in a hurry, but shrugged agreeably. "Okay." She glanced down. "Give me your aunt's name and address, and then I'll read you the insurance stuff."

Gavin dictated the information Meg requested, and by the time the saleswoman returned with the boxed tureen, the form had been completed. When the woman rang up the purchase on the cash register, Gavin took out his wallet and paid for it in cash.

Meg's eyes nearly bugged out of her head when she saw how much cash he was carrying with him. Wasn't he worried about being robbed? Alarmed, she quickly glanced around to see if anyone else had noticed and was relieved to see that the people nearby were involved in their own affairs.

"This should be delivered in three days, sir," the saleswoman told Gavin. "Thank you. Please come again."

Gavin smiled and nodded, then turned to Meg. "I'm getting hungry. How about you?"

She nodded absently as she left the store. Her emotions were involved in a heavy debate with her mind just then. Hunger fell a distant third in priorities.

Should she stick her nose in where it didn't belong? she wondered. Gavin was an adult and his money affairs were his own business, but didn't he realize he was taking a big chance by carrying around so much cash? What if he got pickpocketed? Or mugged? The newspapers were constantly filled with horror stories of people being attacked for far less money than Gavin was carrying. Her own father had had his wallet stolen once. What a mess he'd had straightening out his affairs because of it.

She bit her lip. What should she do? What should she do?

"Meg?" Gavin waved his hand in front of her eyes. "Hello. Hello?"

Startled, she glanced up. She and Gavin were clear across the mall. "Did you say something?"

He nodded, obviously amused by her absentmindedness. "I gave you a list of choices for lunch, but I guess you weren't listening."

"No, I wasn't," she admitted. "I'm sorry, I was thinking about something else. We can eat wherever you want."

"All right." He took her elbow and steered her through the double glass doors. "There's a diner down the road that serves pretty good food. At least, it did a year ago. We can go there."

"Okay."

The sky was still overcast when they got outside, but it had stopped raining. As they walked across the black-topped parking lot to Gavin's pickup, Meg's thoughts wandered back to her dilemma.

"Uh-oh. I can see I'm losing you again," Gavin commented.

Her eyes flew to his. "I'm sorry. I really don't mean to be rude."

He shrugged. "Hey, it's not your fault. I'm obviously boring you. We can skip lunch and go back if you want."

"I'm not bored," she denied, feeling guilty that she'd given him that impression. "I've just been trying to make up my mind about something."

They reached the black pickup and Gavin held open the passenger door. "What's the problem? Maybe I can help."

Meg set her shopping bag on the center of the bench seat, then climbed in and turned to face him. "The problem is that I'm not sure I should say anything."

He frowned. "Wait a second." He shut the passenger door, then walked around and climbed in the driver's side. "You're not sure you should say anything about what to who?" he asked, closing the door.

She sighed. "Something has come to my attention that's none of my business," she said, watching him carefully, "but I feel I should say something, because I'm concerned for that person's well-being."

"You're still talking in riddles," he said, turning the ignition key. The engine leaped to life. "Can't you be more specific?"

She thought for a moment as she adjusted her seat belt and clicked it into place. "I can't be more specific until I know whether or not you feel someone is justified for sticking their nose in where it doesn't belong if they think they have good reason."

Gavin's eyes searched hers as he slid his seat belt across his body into the metal catch. "I can tell that you think you have good reason for whatever we're talking about here. And you obviously care about the person involved, or you wouldn't be so concerned about offending them. If they realize that, they shouldn't hold your nosiness against you." He tilted his head. "Does that answer your question?"

She nodded, smiling weakly.

"Are you still worried about Carol being with Ivan and Kurt?" he asked in a sympathetic tone.

"No." Looking him straight in the eyes, she took a deep breath, releasing it in a rush. "I'm worried about you."

Gavin stiffened. "Me?"

# *Chapter Seven*

"Oh, I knew I shouldn't have said anything," Meg murmured, "but you said you wouldn't hold my nosiness against me."

He didn't answer. He couldn't. He'd known spending time with her would be chancy, but he hadn't thought she'd catch on this quickly. Regretting the sudden turn of events, he backed the pickup out of the parking space and drove toward the exit. The sooner they got back to the circus grounds the better.

"I'm sorry, Gavin."

Her tone was as heavy as his heart, and he couldn't help feeling sorry for both of them, for what they might have had together.

"I just couldn't help seeing all that money in your wallet when you paid for your aunt's present," she went on. "Maybe you'll think I'm paranoid, but I think it's dangerous to carry that much money around with you."

Money? What was she talking about? he wondered. Was it possible he'd misunderstood her and she hadn't found him out?

"Go on," he prompted, anxious to hear that she wasn't talking about the same thing as he was thinking.

Her sigh drew his attention. He glanced over and saw the stubborn tilt of her chin. Her eyes held a hint of reproach.

"Go on," he repeated, turning his attention back to his driving. "I won't bite your head off."

"Well, what if someone stole your wallet? What would you have to live on?" Her voice raised defensively. "And what would happen to Dennis if some unsavory character saw how much money you were carrying and mugged you? Or—Or worse," she added huskily.

Hearing the catch in her voice, Gavin reached across the seat for her hand. He squeezed it gently. "You're right, Meg. I shouldn't be carrying so much money. My only excuse is that after I picked up my pay this morning, I forgot to take some of it out of my wallet." He glanced over at her and smiled, then turned his attention back to the road.

"It's partly your fault, you know," he said.

"My fault?"

He chuckled at the outrage in her voice. "Yes. Partly. If you didn't kiss so damn well, I might have been able to keep my wits about me when I went back to my trailer to change into dry clothes."

"Oh. Sorry," she mumbled.

He laughed and brought the back of her hand up to his lips. Brushing a light kiss over the soft skin, he glanced at her briefly and said, "Don't be. I'm not." No longer interested in rushing back to the show grounds, he turned the pickup into the lot of a small diner and parked.

Once the engine was off, he reached out and stroked her cheek with his knuckles. "Thank you for caring enough to say something." Lightly tweaking her nose, he smiled. "What man could regret having something this pretty stuck into his business?"

Meg sighed in relief. He wasn't angry. She could have sworn that had been his initial reaction. But if he had been, he wasn't now, and she wasn't going to waste any time wondering about what had changed his mind.

Gavin locked the pickup and held her hand as they walked to the restaurant. In a day full of emotional ups and downs, Meg was glad they were back in an "up" period.

Still holding her hand, he opened the thick wooden door. Most of the tables and booths inside were occupied, but there wasn't a waiting line. She was glad. The tantalizing aroma of grilled meat and onions made her mouth water as soon as she walked in.

"There's an empty booth by the window," Gavin said, pulling her right past the Please Wait to be Seated sign. "Let's sit there."

"Oh— Don't you think we should wait until someone seats us?" she asked, glancing back over her shoulder. The man who'd been ringing up a couple's bill at the counter when they'd walked in was scurrying after them with menus.

Gavin stopped next to the booth and turned to the short, dark-haired man who'd come up behind them. "Is it all right if we sit here?"

"Yes, sir." The man's answer was polite, but Meg could tell he was slightly irritated. His smile didn't reach his eyes.

She slid onto the blue vinyl bench across from Gavin and accepted the menu handed to her.

A puzzled frown knit Gavin's brow as he watched the man walk away. "I wonder what his problem is?"

Meg leaned forward. "There was a Wait to be Seated sign by the counter," she quietly informed him. "I think he's upset because we didn't let him seat us."

Gavin's embarrassed blush drew her sympathy. "I didn't notice..." His voice trailed off.

The sign was so large that she didn't know how he'd missed it, but she also knew he was too well mannered to ignore the sign intentionally.

She patted his hands, which were folded on the tabletop over his menu. "Don't worry about it." She opened her menu. "Boy, am I hungry!" Perusing the long list of foods, she couldn't make up her mind. She glanced across at Gavin, who was looking around them.

"Aren't you going to read the menu?" she asked.

He shook his head. "Nope. I already know what I want."

"Oh. How do you know they have it?"

"All family restaurants have cheeseburgers," he said blithely. "I've had a hankering for one ever since you mentioned it earlier."

She smiled. "That does sound pretty good. Maybe I'll have one, too."

"Copycat."

She shrugged and smiled. "Guilty as charged." Closing her menu, she placed it on the white tabletop. "Everything sounds so good, I can't make up my mind." She sniffed as a waitress walked by carrying two plates heaped with spaghetti and meat sauce. "Mmm. Everything *smells* good, too."

"Especially you." Gavin's quiet comment drew her attention. "Your perfume is very attractive."

Meg wasn't sure whether it was the sexy timber of his voice or the intensity of his gaze that caused it, but the air between them suddenly vibrated with awareness. She came back with the first thing that popped into her head.

"Thanks, but anything would be an improvement over my *eau de liniment*, don't you think?"

Gavin laughed and the tension dissipated as quickly as it had come. Only the barest remnant lingered to add a spark of intimacy to their otherwise casual meal.

Meg enjoyed that simple meal with Gavin more than any meal she'd ever had. Obviously the company had a lot to do with it, she admitted to herself. During their lunch, they talked about Dennis, the circus, how she'd combined her hobby as a clown with her career as a teacher, and how his Uncle Henry had taught him to train horses. They even discussed a few current news events, and Meg quickly learned that Gavin had all the qualities she found attractive in a man.

He was good-looking, intelligent, sensitive, well mannered, had a sense of humor, and was as good a listener as he was a conversationalist. What surprised her, though, was how relaxed she felt with him. She'd had trouble stringing three sentences together when she'd gone out on dates with other men. The conversation she'd made had been stilted and sporadic, and she'd rarely been called back a second time by the same man.

Now, though, she was gabbing with Gavin as easily as she did with Carol. What had happened to her shyness? she wondered. And where had this new sense of self-confidence come from? She had no idea. All she knew was that she liked the person she became when she was with Gavin.

They lingered over the apple pie and coffee they ordered for dessert until they'd drunk as many refills as they could hold. Gavin paid the bill while Meg excused herself.

As she applied lipstick in the ladies' washroom, she looked at herself in the mirror. Did she look any different? She felt different. More attractive. More alive. Could she be falling in love? she wondered.

The same old face reflected back, but her eyes held a sparkle she had never noticed before. She smiled. Even as happy as she felt, she wasn't ready to consider her feeling for Gavin anything more than deep "like." Anxious to rejoin him, she quickly ran a brush through her hair.

When they returned to the circus grounds, they discovered that the fishermen had returned early. Dennis came running out of the Cannone's trailer as Gavin was backing his truck up to his trailer.

"Hi, Dad! Hi, Miss Harper! Look what I got." Dressed in his green camouflage rain slicker, the boy held up a large fish.

Meg, who had slipped on her new rain gear, jumped out of the pickup. "Dennis, you caught that? Wow! I'm impressed."

The boy grinned from ear to ear.

Gavin waved to the old man standing in the doorway of the Cannone trailer. "Thanks, Joe!"

The old man waved back, then closed the door, and Gavin herded them into the trailer out of the rain.

"Let's see your fish, Dennis," he said, holding it up to examine it as Meg and the boy hung their raincoats on the wall hooks by the door. "This is very interesting. How did you get it to swim into your net?"

"Aw, I told Grampa Joe you'd figger it out," Dennis said, nodding his head wisely and pointing his finger to emphasize his statement.

"Figure what out?" Meg asked in confusion.

Gavin smiled. "You've been hustled. Dennis didn't catch this fish. There's no mark from a hook."

Meg raised her eyebrows and turned to Dennis.

"Grampa Joe said it would be a good joke," the boy explained. "He bought a couple of fish at the market, 'cause he says that no self 'spectin' fisherman comes home empty-handed. This one's for our dinner."

"Well, your Grampa Joe's joke sure worked on me. I fell for it hook, line and sinker."

Dennis and Gavin both groaned at her pun, and she wrinkled her nose.

"That was bad, wasn't it?" she agreed.

"We'll forgive you if you'll stay and help us eat up this fish," Gavin commented.

Meg couldn't help noticing the surprised look Dennis gave his father. "I will if it's okay with Dennis," she said. "After all, it is his fish."

The child's big brown eyes sparkled in his animated face. "It's okay with me!"

Smiling at his enthusiasm, Meg held out her palm and answered, "All right. Give me five, partner."

Dennis slapped his palm on hers, then flipped his hand over so she could reciprocate.

Gavin smiled. "I'll go clean the fish. Maybe you'd like to show Dennis what we bought him this afternoon."

"Oh, I almost forgot." Meg picked up the bag she'd dropped by the door as Gavin carried the fish off to the kitchen. She handed the bag to Dennis. "Your dad bought you some books while we were shopping."

"Dad bought me books?" The child's tone was so incredulous that Meg couldn't help being shocked.

"Yes. Is that so unusual?"

Dennis didn't answer. He sucked in his lower lip and dropped his gaze to the bag. Pulling out the three books, he shuffled through them. "Neat. Will you read them to me?" he asked, looking up.

She shook her head and smiled. "No. You're going to read them to me. They're easy readers. I'll help you if you have trouble, though." She turned on an end-table lamp, which gave a cozy glow to the room, then sat next to Dennis on the sofa. Still puzzled, she asked, "Didn't your father buy you all your other books?"

He shook his head. "No, Aunt May and Uncle Henry sent them to me for my birthday and Christmas."

"Oh."

"Dad buys me lotsa other stuff, though," he said, quickly coming to his father's defense.

"Of course he does," she assured the boy. Dropping the subject, she asked what he thought about the new books.

"They're awesome." He held up the book with the robot on the cover. "Can I read this one first?"

"Sure."

Dennis opened the book and began reading the words, haltingly at first. Meg gently corrected him, telling him to watch for the punctuation and read the words as sentences, praising him when he did. After a few pages, he folded his blue-jeaned legs and stockinged feet under him and snuggled up to her side. A feeling of tenderness swept through her at the child's unconscious gesture. She placed her arm around his small shoulders.

Sensing that she was being watched a few minutes later, Meg turned her head and saw Gavin standing in the kitchen doorway.

He smiled stiffly, then silently mouthed that he was going out to check on the horses.

She nodded, disappointed. She realized that Gavin probably didn't have much of a choice, since the horses were his responsibility, but she couldn't help feeling that the animals would be fine in the hands of his assistants for another half hour. Dennis was reading so well. She would have liked Gavin to take the time to sit and listen.

Gavin would have liked nothing better than to join Dennis and Meg in the living room, but he knew he couldn't. Seeing his son curled up to Meg's side reading the books she'd picked out for him filled him with so many conflicting emotions, he had to get away. Needing to work off the panicky tension that was tying his stomach in knots, he threw on his slicker and boots. He couldn't get out of the trailer fast enough.

Gavin strode to the horse tent, hunching his shoulders against the driving rain. The inside of the tent was dimly illuminated by a few bare bulbs strung down the center, and he had to step around the small group of men playing poker on a bale of hay.

"Feed the horses yet, Tom?" he asked his sandy-blond assistant.

"Yes, sir," the lounging young man answered around the toothpick stuck between his teeth. "Me 'n Dave 'n Jeff got 'em all shined up and purty, too."

"Good. Thanks," Gavin grunted, wishing that for once his assistants hadn't been so darned efficient. Grooming Ginger would have given him an outlet for his nervous energy, but he wouldn't insult the men by repeating a job they'd already done. Striding down the length of the tent, he saw that the horses had been well cared for, so he slipped out the other end.

Wanting to be alone to think, he wandered toward the lion cages. He stepped under the awning and watched Fatima pacing in her cage. Arturo, her mate, was sound asleep beside her, as were most of the other cats in the long row.

"So, Fatima, want some company?"

The lioness watched him with her golden eyes and continued pacing.

Gavin smiled. Maybe pacing was just what he needed. With hands thrust deep in his pockets, he walked the length of the awning and sorted through the emotions that were tearing him apart.

Seeing Dennis and Meg snuggled together on the sofa had made him feel—what? Happy? Worried? Proud? Envious? All of the above?

Gavin stopped and pushed back his hood. Running his hand through his hair, he turned and retraced his steps.

He was happy and afraid for Dennis at the same time, he decided with a sigh. His son seemed to like Meg a lot, which wasn't surprising. She gave him special attention that he'd never known from another woman. Gavin was glad for Dennis, but what would happen when she left at the end of the summer? Would Dennis be heartbroken?

Could he do anything to keep his son from growing too attached to Meg? he wondered. Gavin knew that he'd made a mistake when he'd invited Meg to dinner. He hadn't been thinking about what was best for Dennis at the time, though. He'd selfishly wanted to spend more time with her. From now on, he'd have to make sure that Dennis only saw Meg during the reading lesson.

Gavin stopped at the other end of the awning and massaged the back of his neck. Facing the other emotions warring inside him wasn't so easy. He'd never felt so high or so low as when he'd heard Dennis reading to Meg.

Turning, he continued to pace. How could he be filled with so much pride and so much envy at the same time? he wondered. He loved his son more than anything or anyone on earth. He wanted the best for Dennis. He wanted him to be able to hold his head up high and never have to worry about hiding the reality of who or what he was. The world would be Dennis's for the taking if he knew how to read.

So how come he'd had to bite his tongue to keep from interrupting the cozy scene of Dennis reading to Meg? Why had he turned and fled instead of staying to admire his son's accomplishment?

Guilt gnawed at his stomach and he swallowed the bile that rose in his throat. Was he actually envious of his own son?

"No!"

Two lions jumped up in their cages and snarled, surprising Gavin. He hadn't realized he'd spoken aloud.

"Down, boys. Down. Everything's okay," he said in a soothing tone. Knowing he was the source of the cats' irritation, he turned and walked away to the other end.

He wasn't envious of his son, he decided. His pride had just been stung because Dennis, who had always looked up to him, was now able to do something he wasn't able to. *And* Gavin had felt like an outsider, not a new experience by any means, but definitely a new experience where his son was concerned. Dennis had just taken his first step toward independence, toward not needing his father.

The panic Gavin felt now wasn't so strong, now that he knew he was just facing a reality of life all parents had to face. Breaking apron strings, that's what it was. Unpleasant, but unavoidable.

He stopped in front of Fatima, who was still pacing, and smiled. "Your medicine worked for me. How are you doing?"

"Hey! Gavin, *mon ami*, is there a problem?" Jacques came jogging around the corner of the cages. The black slicker he'd thrown on flapped open, revealing his gray sweatpants and bare chest. His worried frown relaxed as his gaze skimmed down the line of cats.

"No, there's no problem," Gavin quickly assured him. "I was just doing some thinking out loud and woke up a couple of your lazy cats. They didn't like it."

"Lazy cats, you say? Hmph. Zay have more sense zan you, it seems." Jacques scowled. "Sleeping is ze much smarter way to spend ze day off zan walking around in ze rain."

Gavin noticed his friend's messy hair and unshaven face. "Sorry. Did I wake you?"

"No, but I was in bed." Jacques nodded over his shoulder to the cage where the sleeping Arturo had woken up and engaged Fatima in an activity other than pacing. "Arturo's got ze right idea." Jacques's dark eyes gleamed as he waggled his eyebrows. "Monique is probably pacing ze floor waiting for me. Go find yourself a woman, *mon ami*," Jacques advised, walking away. "Making love will make you feel like you can tackle any problem."

Gavin shook his head and laughed, then walked back through the rain toward his trailer. "Making love would add to my problems, my friend," he said, talking quietly to himself. The only woman he had any interest in making love to was strictly off limits. He had to figure out how to *resist* kissing her, touching her, spending time with her.

Meg and Dennis were sitting in the middle of the floor playing Pick Up Sticks when he opened the door. His son looked up.

"Hi, Dad! Guess what! I read the whole robot book." He glanced quickly at Meg and added, "With a little help."

Gavin removed his boots and hung up his slicker. "I heard you reading. You did a good job, pal." Walking over to Dennis, he crouched down and hugged him. "I'm sorry I had to miss it. Maybe you can read your book to me later before you go to bed. Okay?"

"Okay! It's a funny story. You'll really like it." Dennis turned to Meg, who hadn't said anything. "Won't he?"

She nodded, but Gavin noticed her lips quivered when she smiled. Were those tears he saw in the corners of her eyes?

She ducked her head and he stood up, not wanting to acknowledge her softhearted reaction. He couldn't resist her if she had teary eyes.

He looked at Dennis. "How do you want your fish cooked, buddy?"

"Fried in that crunchy batter," came the instant reply. "With lotsa tartar sauce to dip it in."

Gavin smiled. "I shouldn't have bothered asking."

"And can you make those tiny fried potatoes, too?" Dennis added.

"Hash browns?" Gavin paused in the kitchen doorway and made a face. "That's an awful lot of grease there, kiddo."

"Aw, pleeeease?"

Gavin glanced at Meg and was glad to see she'd regained her composure. "Is that okay with you, Meg?"

She looked up at him, then glanced at Dennis. His son's eyes had the pleading puppy expression with which he was quite familiar, and he knew what Meg's answer would be before she replied.

"Sure. That's fine," she answered. "Can I help you do anything?"

"No, thanks. You stay and finish your game with Dennis. I'll take care of dinner."

Gavin worked quickly, anxious to get the meal on the table. The sooner they ate, the sooner Meg would leave. Then he could start bolstering his defenses and work out some type of plan of resistance and avoidance for the future.

In the three weeks that followed, Meg looked upon her first meal with Gavin and Dennis as "the last supper." She sensed a change in Gavin's attitude toward her after that day. She wasn't invited out by him again, even though she knew he spent his days off alone, as Dennis always mentioned when he was going fishing with Grampa Joe.

She continued to give Dennis his reading lesson every afternoon, at which Gavin was always present. Knowing that Dennis wasn't shy, she was unable to think of a reason for his father's attendance. *Unless* he wanted to be with her. But then why didn't he ever seek her out during any of their free time?

Gavin was friendly and pleasant during her riding lessons, but nothing more. No kisses. No touches. No intimate glances. Was she crazy? She couldn't have imagined his interest and attraction that first week.

So what happened? she wondered. What had she done on that day of their first and last date that had turned him off?

It was always at this point in her introspection that Meg's heart stopped—as she remembered when Gavin had walked in after checking the horses, congratulated Dennis on his reading and asked his son to read to him later. She got misty-eyed whenever she remembered the love shining between father and son.

Each time she asked herself if Gavin could possibly have detected that that moment had changed her life. Could he have known that that had been the moment she'd realized she was falling in love with a man who traveled for a living and a little boy who smelled like fish?

Each time her answer was ''no.'' She'd been very careful not to look at him until she'd composed herself. He wasn't a mind reader. He couldn't have figured out her secret.

So why had he pulled back just when they'd started growing so close? She had no answer.

By mid-July, the circus had wound its way out of Wisconsin, into Iowa, back through Illinois, and on into Indiana. The weather had been hot, but pleasant, and Meg had gotten used to the routine of going to bed late, after the big top came down, then rising early to travel and set the big top back up. Napping at free moments became a common occurrence, and she wondered how long it would take her to change around to her old sleeping habits once she went back to teaching.

Meg had gotten to know most of the show people fairly well, the circus being like one big extended family. Carol, being so outgoing, had helped her make friends within the close-knit group. Having few living relatives, Meg enjoyed the feeling of belonging.

Carol was having a good time with Kurt and Ivan, who'd appointed themselves as her guides. She'd invited Meg to go along with them to the Indiana dunes one day, and Meg had gone. The Alexander brothers had regaled them with outrageous stories of their travels with a European circus, but Meg wondered how much of what they said was true and how much was made up. Kurt and Ivan were constantly trying to upstage each other, and Meg had quickly tired of their boisterous bragging. By the end of the day she had a giant-size headache, due as much to an overdose of their incessant chatter as to too much sun.

The day had one redeeming moment, though. She ran into Gavin on the way back to her trailer and he asked how she was feeling.

"Awful," she answered, shading her eyes against the glare of the setting sun. "I have a terrible headache."

"And a terrible sunburn. Do you have anything to put on it?"

"Carol's getting something at the drugstore. Right now I'm more worried about my head. Excuse me, I have to go take a couple of aspirin and lay down." She climbed into her camper, but a few minutes later there was a knock at the door.

"Come in," she called, too ill to get up from her bed.

Gavin entered with an ice pack and a tube of sunburn ointment. "I thought you might want to borrow these."

Grateful, she reached for the ice pack and pressed it to her forehead, replacing the wet washcloth that had already grown warm. "Thanks. You're a lifesaver," she whispered. "My head is pounding so bad it hurts to talk."

Gavin removed the washcloth from her hands. "Then don't talk," he said quietly. "Just close your eyes and relax. I'll put the ointment on for you."

"Thanks," she whispered, hurting too much to worry about the propriety of him seeing her in her cotton baby-doll pajamas.

Kneeling on the floor next to her bed, he gently smoothed the ointment over her sunburned arms and legs, then had her turn on her side, so he could get to her back.

She held her breath when he reached under her loose top and applied the salve to her back and shoulders. She'd never been touched so intimately by a man. One thing good about being sunburned, she decided, was that it covered her blush.

He smoothed down her top, then stroked the back of her neck with the ointment. His fingers massaged away some of the ache inside her head, and she sighed.

"Does that feel good?" he asked huskily.

"Yes. Please don't stop," she whispered. "It helps."

He kneaded the back of her neck until they heard the approach of voices. "Sounds like Carol's back," he whispered.

Her friend's high-pitched laugh mingled with Kurt and Ivan's loud guffaws and Meg put her hands over her ears.

"Do they have to be so loud?" she groaned. With her eyes shut in agony, she sensed, rather than saw, Gavin's movement.

He rose, saying, "I'll take care of it. You stay in bed for the rest of the night. I'll tell Nate you're too sick to take down the big top."

"Thanks." She rolled from her side to her back, and felt the quick brush of his lips on her temple.

"A kiss to make it better," he whispered, making her feel very precious. He left and spoke to the loud trio in hushed tones, getting them to settle down, to Meg's everlasting gratitude.

Carol tiptoed in to check on her, then left her in peace.

Sometime later Meg fell asleep, content that Gavin cared for her. She wasn't sure how much, or in what way, but he wasn't indifferent, of that she was sure. All she had to do was break through the wall he'd built up between them. She had six weeks left with the circus. She hoped it would be enough time.

## Chapter Eight

Three days later, the circus had crossed over into Ohio. Meg hadn't made any further progress in her relationship with Gavin, but she had caught him staring at her on a few occasions. Was that longing she detected in his eyes? Or only wishful thinking on her part?

That morning after breakfast, Meg and Carol met in the big top to rehearse a new routine in front of two other clowns. Carol had gotten wind of Meg's snake phobia via Rosa Cannone and thought it would make a great idea for a routine. Meg had gone along with the idea, thinking that if she ever wanted to get over her phobia she had to do something about it. Getting used to the large inflatable snake Carol purchased in the garden center of a discount store was Meg's first positive step toward overcoming her fear.

They had just finished rehearsing, when they heard a commotion out on the midway.

"I wonder what that's all about?" Carol asked, props in hand. "Go see. I'll put this stuff away."

"Okay." Meg walked out the main entrance, squinting her eyes against the bright sunlight.

"Look out!" a male voice shouted.

Meg froze as several large boys on bicycles whizzed by on each side of her. The teenagers taunted and laughed at the three men chasing them on foot. The last boy in the wild procession bumped Meg as he flew past, his shoulder knocking her off balance into the dirt.

"Get out of here!" shouted Gavin's assistant Tom, who paused to help Meg up as Dave and Jeff continued the chase. "Are you all right, ma'am?"

"Yes, thanks," she said, dusting off her derriere.

"*Madre de Dios!*" Rosa Cannone's voice behind her made Meg cringe. Wherever Rosa was, Lucky was not far away. Meg had gotten used to seeing the snake draped around Rosa's shoulders, but always from a distance. Close up was another story.

"Meg, are you okay?" the woman asked, concern apparent in her tone.

Meg turned warily.

Rosa held up her hands. "Don't worry. I left Lucky with Rico."

"Thank you, Rosa. I'm fine. Just a little dirty."

The dark-haired woman shook her head as she gazed after the teenagers. "Bicycles on the midway." She clucked her tongue. "This is bad." Making the sign of the cross, the woman looked at Meg sympathetically and hugged her. "You be careful. Bicycles on the midway is a bad omen."

Not wanting to offend the superstitious woman, Meg didn't tell her she didn't believe in omens. "Thank you, Rosa. I will."

Gavin came out of the office trailer not far from where they were standing, and Rosa called to him.

"Gavin, did you see? Bicycles on the midway! They knocked Meg down."

His eyes narrowed and he hurried down the wooden steps. "Meg, are you all right?"

"Yes, yes, I'm fine," she assured him, growing embarrassed by all the attention. "I just fell down and got a little dirty. No harm's been done. It's not that big a deal."

"We'll see how big a deal it is," Rosa said ominously. "You know what happened two weeks ago."

"Do you mean when Rico broke his arm?" Meg asked.

"Yes, my poor baby. It was all that new guy George's fault. He was whistling in the big top when he was adjusting the rigging."

"What—"

"Rico was playing hide-and-seek down below," Gavin explained, anticipating her question.

"Whistling is very bad luck," said Rosa. "So are bicycles on the midway. You be careful. I do not wish what happened to my Rico to happen to you."

"She'll be careful," Gavin assured Rosa. "I'll watch over her to make sure."

"Good." Rosa nodded, as if that was settled, and turned. "Uh-oh. The bad luck has started already."

Meg and Gavin turned around to see what she was talking about. A police officer was knocking on the door of the office trailer. The three stood and warily watched Nathan Marshall and the officer converse in the open doorway.

Though she couldn't hear what the policeman was telling Nate, Meg knew it wasn't good. Nate's scowling face grew a darker and darker shade of red, a barometer of his anger.

Nate's gaze lit on the trio and his voice boomed, "Has anyone seen Barnett?"

Alvin Barnett, Meg knew, was the elephant trainer. He was a funny old codger, who cosseted his "girls," as he called the elephants, like princesses. Meg liked the odd little man and hoped he wasn't in trouble.

"He's still at the dentist because of that abscessed tooth," Gavin replied, striding forward. "What's the problem, Nate?"

"One of the damn bulls got loose and is tearing up some woman's garden."

"Which way?"

"South of here, about a half mile," replied the police-man. "Redbrick house along the main highway. But it's an elephant that's loose, not a bull."

"A bull is an elephant, officer," Meg explained with a gentle smile. "I was confused at first, too, so don't feel bad."

"It's probably Alice again. Do you want me to bring her back?" Gavin asked Nate.

"Yeah, you'd better get over there as fast as you can be-fore she does any more damage. I'll be right along."

"You be careful, Gavin," Rosa said with a frown. "The way things are goin'—"

"I'll go, too," Meg volunteered. "I'll make sure nothing bad happens to him, Rosa."

Gavin smiled and grabbed her hand, pulling her along behind him as he jogged away. He pulled a set of keys from his jeans pocket and thrust them into her palm. "Here. Go get my pickup. I've got to get a bull hook. Meet me out be-hind the cook house."

"Okay." Meg sprinted toward the performers' trailers, making a brief stop to pick up her purse before running to Gavin's pickup. Her heart felt like it had sprouted wings and was ready to fly. She and Gavin were going to round up an elephant together. How exciting! And how interesting that he trusted her to drive his pickup. And how *wonderful* that he'd smiled at her and held her hand! Things were looking up.

She picked Gavin up behind the cook house. He climbed in the passenger side, letting her drive.

"It's Alice that's loose, all right," he informed her as she drove toward the main road. "She freed herself of her leg shackles. The kid Alvin left to watch over them was sound asleep in the hay. I'd hate to be him when Alvin gets back." He turned his face toward her. "By the way, thanks for vol-unteering to come along," he said. "I needed someone to drive my pickup back to the grounds."

"And you needed someone to watch over you so you don't have any bad luck," Meg teased, turning onto the main highway.

"Yeah, that, too." Gavin grinned.

"Well, you volunteered to watch over me. The least I could do was reciprocate." She shook her head. "I find it hard to understand how anyone can really believe all that superstitious stuff."

He shrugged. "It's a way some people explain things they don't have a reason for."

She glanced his way. "You don't believe it, do you?"

"No, not really." He paused, then raised his eyebrows. "There have been times that I've wondered, though. Sometimes things happen—well, the coincidence is there."

Meg spotted the redbrick house among the other houses spread out along the highway, and pulled the pickup onto the long, gravel driveway.

"Like what?" she asked, wondering what had happened to make him unsure.

"Well, there were kids riding bicycles on the midway the day my wife left." Gavin's wry smile pulled at her heart.

"You don't think that's why—" she began.

"No, I know that's not why she left," he scoffed. "Lydia found someone she liked better."

"Better than you?" The woman had to be out of her mind, Meg thought.

"Yeah, well, I'm no bargain," he said quietly. "And Lydia was very ambitious."

"Was she a performer?"

"Yes. She was a belly dancer in the sideshow. She counted on her beauty to get her ahead, which I guess it did. She took off with a magician and worked as his assistant for a while. I was the last to know that something had been going on between them for several months before they left the circus." He shrugged, but Meg could tell he was just attempting to cover his hurt.

"By the time our divorce became final," he continued, "Lydia had already left him for some rich gambler she'd met in Atlantic City."

"What about Dennis?" Meg asked as she stopped the pickup in front of the white garage doors.

He sighed. "Our son was an accident she never wanted any part of. Needless to say, she was more than happy to give me full custody."

"Does she visit him?"

"No. She hasn't seen him since the day she left." Frowning, Gavin reached for the door handle. "I'd better go get Alice. Thanks for driving me over." He got out of the truck and strode around the side of the garage.

With a heart made heavy by Gavin's story, Meg followed him, too apprehensive to leave just yet. She wanted to make sure he didn't have any trouble getting the elephant to obey him. Meg knew he was familiar with the elephants, since she'd seen him leading an elephant when the big top was raised and lowered, but she was concerned that he wouldn't be able to control Alice in unfamiliar surroundings.

Besides, she was curious to see what kind of havoc the elephant had wreaked on the unsuspecting neighborhood. Entering the backyard, she saw that there was, indeed, an elephant in the small vegetable garden. She couldn't help laughing at the sight of the large pachyderm munching the elephant-size salad it had found.

Noticing a movement from the corner of her eye, Meg saw a young blond woman peeking out the back door of the house. She held a baby in her arms. A wide-eyed little girl of about four had her nose pressed up against the window next to the door.

"Are you from the circus?" the woman asked.

"Yes," Meg answered, walking up to her. "I'm sorry the elephant wrecked your garden. I hope you can salvage some of it. The owner of the circus will be here soon to talk to you."

"All right. Is it safe to come outside? My little girl is dying to get a closer look."

Meg smiled. The woman had every right to be angry, but she was obviously more thrilled with the novelty of having an elephant in her yard. "Let me check. I'll be right back."

Meg walked toward Gavin, who was steering the elephant out of the garden. She stopped a short distance away. "The lady's not mad at all," she said quietly.

Gavin raised his brows. "Nate'll be glad to hear that."

"She wants to know if her little girl can get a closer look. Is it safe?"

"Sure, she can get a closer look. Just let me get Alice away from all this temptation first. Alice, forward," he commanded, stopping the elephant when they reached the middle of the lawn.

Meg ran back and told the woman she could bring her daughter outside.

"Can I pet it, Mommy?" the little girl asked.

"I don't know, Wendy," the mother said warily. "It's awfully big."

"I can hold your little girl up out of harm's way, if she wants to pet the elephant," Gavin volunteered.

"You wouldn't mind?"

"Not at all."

"Gee, I'd love to get a picture of this. Is it okay if I run inside and get my camera?"

"Sure."

A worried-looking Nate Marshall showed up just as the woman was snapping a photo of Gavin holding her daughter up to pet Alice. Meg, holding the baby, stood next to Gavin so the woman could get both her children in the shot.

"The elephant's name is Alice," Gavin explained to the little girl. "Pet her right up here on her shoulder. That's a girl. She likes that. Alice likes making new friends."

Hearing Gavin talk quietly with the little girl, Meg beamed. Gavin was so wonderful with children, she thought. He was a terrific father. She couldn't help feeling he'd also be a terrific husband. His ex-wife had to have a personality problem, Meg decided. That she could have preferred anyone else over this kind, gentle, loving man was unthinkable.

Meg tipped her head and frowned in concentration as she suddenly recalled the incident that happened at breakfast over a month ago, when she'd returned Kurt's unwanted hand to his own lap. Gavin's misreading of the situation had seemed odd at the time, but now it made more sense. His assumption that she wanted to get to know Kurt better could have been a reaction to his past with Lydia. Meg had thought she'd set Gavin straight about what happened, but maybe he hadn't believed her. Knowing his wife had played around behind his back must have hurt his ego. Was that why he'd been keeping his distance, she wondered?

Several other people began showing up with their children, neighbors of the woman in the redbrick house, who asked if they could take pictures, too. Nate's grin widened with pleasure. Even a local newspaper reporter showed up for a picture and a story. What could have been a fiasco for the circus suddenly turned into a great bit of publicity. Nate gave the woman from the redbrick house free tickets to that evening's performance and monetary compensation for the loss of her vegetable garden before they parted ways, and Gavin guided Alice back the way she'd come.

Meg frowned thoughtfully as she drove back to the circus grounds. Gavin had so much love to give, but he'd obviously been hurt. She couldn't blame him for being wary of getting involved with someone else. After being burned, it must be awfully hard to trust again.

Meg smiled wryly. Placing your trust in someone was tough enough the first time. She was falling in love with Gavin, but she was afraid to tell him. Could he possibly care for her, too, and be afraid to tell her? She sighed. She knew she couldn't ask him. If he said "no," she'd be crushed. If he said "yes," what would happen then? Would they get married and live happily ever after? In a traveling circus? That certainly wasn't her idea of heaven, but what if it was his? Did she love him enough to give up her house and live the gypsy life in a trailer? She didn't know. Deciding that it was premature to consider such thoughts, she turned on the radio for distraction.

Arriving back at the circus grounds, Meg parked the pickup, then strolled over to wait for Gavin where the elephants were staked out. The metal leg shackles clanked endlessly as the elephants swayed and pulled against them. Meg had gotten used to the noise, but today a thumping vibration accompanied the metallic sound. The elephants were rolling their trunks and thumping them on the ground and fanning their large ears.

"What's going on?" she asked the sleepy-looking young man, who was brushing one of the large beasts.

"Storm's a-comin'," he replied. "Did Gavin find Alice?"

"Yes. They should be back here soon."

The young man's scrawny shoulders heaved with his sigh of relief and his eyes raised heavenward. "Thankee kindly, Lawd. I'm 'bliged."

Meg smiled sympathetically. She hoped for the young man's sake that Gavin and Alice arrived before Alvin Barnett got back from the dentist.

"Joe Bob! Where the hell's Alice?" Alvin Barnett's raspy voice startled Meg, and she spun around.

"It's okay, Mr. Barnett," she quickly answered, holding up her palms defensively as the young Joe Bob cowered behind her. "Gavin's got her. They went for a little walk, but they'll be back here any minute." Her eyes scanned the open field beyond the circus grounds. "Look! Here they come now. See! Alice is fine."

Alvin's dark beady eyes focused on Gavin and the elephant walking beside him like a hawk's on his prey. The old man didn't say a word, but his scowl spoke volumes. He strode swiftly toward the two, and Meg had to run to keep up. The way Alvin's fists were clenched, she was afraid he was going to punch Gavin.

She jumped between the two, once again holding up her palms to ward the old man off.

"What the hell's goin' on here, Gavin? What're you doin' with Alice?"

The elephant reached out to her trainer with her trunk, and he patted her protectively. Alvin's eyes swept back and forth between Gavin and the elephant, as if he couldn't decide whether he wanted to stare Gavin down, or check to make sure his precious Alice was all right.

"Calm down, Alvin," Gavin replied in a soothing tone. "Your bull got loose and decided to ransack some woman's garden, that's all. Alice is fine. I just went to fetch her."

"Alice got loose? Damn! Where the hell was Joe Bob?"

"The kid fell asleep, and before you go tannin' his hide, remember St. Louis last year."

Alvin frowned. "Yes, okay. I get you."

Gavin smiled. "Besides, everything worked out just fine. Nate talked to the woman and gave her some free tickets to the show. Here. You take Alice back," he said, holding out the bull hook.

Alvin fixed his beady gaze on Meg. "You can get outa my way now, missy. I ain't gonna hit him. Never was."

Meg stepped aside, feeling sheepish. "Sorry. You looked like you were going to," she defended.

"An' I s'pose you think you coulda stopped me if I was."

She raised her chin. "I would have tried."

"Hmph." Alvin looked at Gavin. "Brave woman," he muttered grudgingly, then turned and led his elephant away. "Shame on you, you naughty girl," he groused, shoving Alice's trunk away stubbornly as the elephant seemed to try to hug him in apology.

Bemused, Meg watched the two walk away and asked Gavin what happened in St. Louis.

"Alice broke her leg shackle and got into a tray of cotton candy."

"Cotton candy! Where was Alvin?"

Gavin grinned conspiratorially. "Asleep."

"Ohh." Meg chuckled, sharing the joke, then dug the keys to Gavin's pickup from her jeans pocket. "Here," she said, holding them out.

He grasped her whole hand, and she glanced up in surprise.

His intense gaze took her breath away. "Why did you jump between Alvin and me like that?"

Meg blushed. "Well, I couldn't let him hit you. It wasn't your fault Alice got loose."

"So you decided I needed defending, even though I'm probably a good six inches taller than Alvin."

She looked away from the amusement twinkling in his eyes, and glanced at her shoes. "I guess that was pretty silly—"

His fingers tilted up her chin, forcing her gaze back to his. "Actually I think it's the nicest thing anyone has done for me in a long time. Thank you." His eyes held hers captive, and she saw that he really was touched that she'd defended him.

"You're welcome," she whispered huskily. Her heart beat wildly, wondering if he would kiss her. The look in his eyes said he wanted to, and she waited breathlessly, but his kiss never came. Instead, he glanced away and shoved his keys into his pocket.

Meg turned, hiding her disappointment. "I—I guess we'd better get back. It's just about time for Dennis's reading lesson."

Gavin cleared his throat behind her. "Right."

For the rest of the day, he treated her with the same friendly distance he'd assumed for the past several weeks. Meg ground her teeth in frustration.

Gavin sat in on Dennis's reading lesson and mended more socks and sewed on more buttons, and Meg wondered if he was hiring out, or pulling off the buttons as an excuse to sit at the kitchen table with them. No one had *that* much mending. She didn't say anything, though, for fear that he'd stop attending.

Recently their riding lessons were not so much lessons, as just riding. Gavin had taught her to ride, but he'd never mentioned discontinuing the sessions now that he'd fulfilled his part of the bargain. Meg was glad.

That night, Carol and Meg performed their new routine for the first time. Carol's demure clown character, Pansy, while on a camping trip, grows tired of playing servant to Meg's demanding Big Bertha character and retaliates by hiding a snake in Big Bertha's sleeping bag. Big Bertha, who hates snakes, runs away in fright, and pleads with Pansy to get rid of the snake for her. Pansy agrees, but not until she extracts Big Bertha's promise to wait on her hand and foot in exchange.

Pleased by the audience's applause and laughter, Carol and Meg ran off to get their props for their next act. The wind whipped at their costumes as they exited the back door, and Meg pulled up short. The elephants were psychic, it seemed. A storm was on the way, though it hadn't yet begun to rain.

A smiling Gavin, dressed in the flashy red-sequined jacket and black pants he wore for his equestrian act, gave her a thumbs-up sign as he awaited his cue in the backyard.

Meg waved and executed a quick bow, pleased by his reaction to their new act. The white Arabian stallion he rode stamped nervously as the canvas door flap ruffled in the wind, but Gavin kept the horse under control. Were all the animals nervous about this storm? she wondered. The lions had seemed unusually high-strung, forcing Jacques to give a shortened performance.

A frisson of foreboding shot down her spine, and she wondered if Rosa's superstitious talk was getting to her.

By the middle of the second show, the wind had grown tremendously and the rain had hit. Bo, the performers' boss, spread the word that the show was going to end early. Several acts were cut, and everyone was told to be on hand to take down the big top as soon as it was cleared.

Meg and Carol stripped off their costumes in clown alley with the rest of the clowns, but left on their makeup. There wasn't time for minor details like that right now. It normally took two hours to take the big top down. The strength of the gusting wind could do untold damage to the canvas if they didn't hurry.

Meg's heart flew up into her throat when she hurried inside the large tent. Gavin was up high, helping to dismantle the rigging that had to come down before the big top could be lowered. She'd never seen him perform this job before and thought this wasn't a very good time for him to be doing something with which he was unfamiliar. What if he lost his balance?

Holding her breath, she watched the way the canvas kept lifting. She knew that if it weren't for the jumper ropes on the quarter poles, the wind would lift the canvas, pulling the poles right out of their sockets.

Meg looked away, filled with a renewed urgency. Rushing past the forklift carting away a load of bleacher lumber, she joined several others who were unlacing the side canvas. Everyone knew that without the big top, they wouldn't have much of a circus, so they all worked quickly and efficiently.

Rosa Cannone, who would normally be taking down the sideshow tent, was helping. "Meg, you see? More bad luck."

Meg didn't answer. With Gavin up high, she didn't want to think about bad luck and bad omens. She believed in positive thinking. Gavin would be all right, she told herself. He was strong. He was well coordinated. He'd be fine.

Still, she couldn't help glancing over her shoulder every now and then to check on him.

Once everything had been cleared from under the big top, George Pepperdine, the circus manager, shouted out the orders, "The big top is coming down! Bring up the trucks and the elephants! Let's move!"

Everyone heaved a sigh of relief once the canvas was down. Many people stayed to fold it so it could be rolled onto the spool truck, while others began dismantling the midway booths and smaller tents.

Meg and Carol helped with the sideshow tent. Working beside Rosa, Meg fought the urge to point out to the superstitious woman that for all her ominous threats of bad luck, everything was working out just fine. Thankful that Gavin was now safely on the ground, Meg decided she could afford to be benevolent.

The sideshow canvas had just come down when Meg heard a shout behind her. The wind was whistling so loudly in her ears that she didn't hear what was said. She turned around, and suddenly everything went black.

With his head down, Gavin was fighting his way to the office trailer through the wind and driving rain to report in to Nate when he heard a shout. Turning in the middle of the dim midway, he witnessed a sight that made his blood run cold. The wind had caught a section of one of the midway booths, and the sheet of plywood was now careening toward the people taking down the sideshow tent.

"Hey! Watch it!" His feet were moving toward them before he got out all the words. Several workers ducked out of the way, but one just turned. Oh, God. He recognized that yellow raincoat.

"Meg!" His heart stopped as he saw the wood strike her in the head. She crumpled instantly. "Meg!"

He kept running, then pushed his way through the group that had gathered around her.

Meg was sitting up, pressing a bandanna to her brow. Clancy, the head clown, was kneeling beside her. His arm was supporting her shoulders.

Gavin dropped to his knees opposite him. "Are you all right?"

"Yes," she said in a weak voice. "A little woozy, though. Did you get the license number of that truck?"

Relieved that she was well enough to joke, Gavin smiled.

"She's got a gash along one side of her forehead," Clancy informed him, tying another bandanna around her brow. "We'd better get her to the infirmary and take a better look."

Gavin picked her up with Clancy's help, then carried her to the office trailer, where one small cubicle held emergency medical supplies. Accidents were commonplace enough around the circus that everyone usually took them in stride, so most people went back to work folding the sideshow tent. Carol followed the trio to the infirmary.

"Will she be okay?" Carol asked in a strangled voice as Gavin gently laid Meg down on the cot.

Gavin couldn't answer. The sight of the blood-soaked fabric sent his heart into his throat.

Clancy, who'd been a medic in the army before joining the circus, washed his hands, and answered a noncommittal, "We'll see."

Gavin stood back and watched Clancy lift the bandanna. The two-inch gash along Meg's hairline was bleeding profusely, and Gavin had a hard time not looking away.

Meg swore out loud as Clancy cleansed the wound, and Gavin grabbed her hands when she tried to push Clancy away.

"Be still, Meg," he said quietly, relieved that she was acting feisty instead of faint.

She focused on him. "Easy for you to say."

Carol hovered at the foot of the cot. "Are you okay, Meggie?"

"Yes, but my head hurts like heck."

"You'll have to go to the hospital for stitches, Meg," said Clancy. "The cut is deep."

"I'll drive you," Gavin stated. He couldn't rest until he knew she was all right.

"I'll come, too," Carol volunteered.

Gavin smiled at Meg's petite friend. "Great. Carol, why don't you go get the directions to the nearest hospital from Nate while I go get my pickup?"

"Okay." Carol left the room as Clancy pressed a sterile dressing to Meg's cut, then wrapped her head with a gauze bandage.

"I'll be right back, Meg." Gavin squeezed the small hands that were still folded in his. She smiled at him.

Driving Meg to the hospital ten minutes later, Gavin squeezed the steering wheel in frustration. Carol had the directions written on a piece of paper, and kept telling him the names of the streets where he had to turn. Being unable to read the street signs, hearing the names did him no good.

He'd already missed one street and had had to turn around to go back.

"Carol, when we get to Midlothian, just tell me, okay?"

"All right. I'm sorry, Gavin, but I really thought you'd seen the sign back at Market Street."

Her tone of voice indicated she didn't know how he'd missed it, and he pressed his lips together to keep from coming up with another excuse. He'd already used one when he'd almost missed the turn back at Tippecanoe Road. Watching traffic had been a flimsy excuse, since there were very few cars on the road, but it had been all he could think of at the spur of the moment.

His gaze slid sideways to Meg, who was seated between them on the bench seat of his pickup. She was frowning as she held the ice pack against her forehead, but he wasn't sure if her expression was due to pain or puzzlement. Was she trying to figure out how he could have missed the sign as well?

They made it to the hospital without further incident, since Carol warned him when he'd have to turn left or right, and Gavin sighed in relief. He wasn't worried about the trip back. He'd watched for landmarks at each of the turns.

At the hospital, the doctor checked Meg and stitched her wound. He thought she'd be all right, but wanted her to take it easy for a few days and had Carol promise to wake her every few hours for the rest of the night.

The trio arrived back at the dark circus grounds a few hours after they'd left. The storm clouds had moved on, the rain had stopped and the wind had died down to a soft breeze. The only light besides that cast by the pickup's headlights was coming from the moon. The animals had been loaded and the equipment packed for the move into Pennsylvania in a few short hours, and everyone appeared to be asleep.

Gavin walked Meg and Carol back to their camper with a flashlight to make sure they didn't trip on anything in the dim light.

"Boy, I'll be glad to get into bed," Carol said wearily, climbing up into the camper.

"I'll be right in," Meg said, closing the door behind her friend. She turned to Gavin. "Thank you for taking me to the hospital."

He smiled. "I can't really say that it was my pleasure, but driving you was no problem."

"It was an awfully long wait," she said quietly. "You could have been sleeping all this time. I'm sorry."

"No, you don't understand. It wasn't the wait I minded."

Her eyes searched his, questioning, and he pulled her into his arms. He couldn't help it. He had held back for as long as he could. He needed to hold her, needed to touch the woman he'd been worried would be taken from him forever by a power he had no control over.

"It was you getting hurt that I minded," he said, his voice a husky whisper. He'd never forget the fear that had shot through him when he had seen her get struck by that sheet of plywood. Having her alive and well and in his arms made his chest tighten with an ache. Gavin bent and kissed her gently on the lips, then released her and backed away before he started putting into words all the sweet longings he was feeling inside.

"Good night, Meg. I'll see you in the morning."

She looked as though she wanted to say something, but then she turned away and climbed into the camper.

Gavin returned to his trailer, where Angela Cannone, Rico's grandmother, was sound asleep on the couch. He touched the old woman's shoulder gently. "Angela, I'm back."

She sat up, rubbing the sleep from her eyes. "How is the teacher—Meg? She is okay?"

Gavin nodded. "Yes, the doctor thinks she'll be fine. She just has to rest for a few days."

Angela studied him with her sharp-eyed gaze. "And you— How are *you?*"

"Me? What makes you think anything's wrong with me?"

She shook her head. "You no fool me. When you care for someone, their troubles are your troubles. I'm *old* woman. Not stupid."

Gavin smiled wryly and helped her up from the couch. "I know that." He hugged her. "You're a very wise woman, but sometimes—" he lightly tapped her nose "—you put this where it doesn't belong."

Angela shrugged her frail shoulders and smiled. "Only because I care."

"I know you do. Now, you'd better get off to bed, or Joe will be after me for having his woman out so late."

He walked her to the door of the Cannone trailer, which was next to his. "Thank you for staying with Dennis."

She gestured with her hand that it was nothing and climbed the steps.

Back in his own trailer, Gavin laid awake in bed thinking about Angela's words. *When you care about someone, their troubles become your troubles.* He cared about Meg, that was for sure, but dealing with her troubles wasn't the problem. Because he cared for her, he didn't want her to have to deal with *his* problems. It wouldn't be fair to her.

Gavin flipped onto his stomach and punched his pillow, trying to get comfortable. Only another five weeks, he thought. Then she'd be gone and he wouldn't have to deal with his conflicting emotions any longer.

He turned onto his side, hugging his pillow. Why didn't the thought bring him any peace?

## Chapter Nine

Meg spent the next morning in bed. She had a slight headache, so her mother hen, Carol, wouldn't allow her out. Meg thought her headache stemmed more from a restless night of tossing and turning and thinking about Gavin than from her head injury, but she didn't feel up to discussing everything with Carol, so she accepted the inactivity forced upon her. Now that she'd grown used to getting up before the crack of dawn, she couldn't sleep and laid in bed, listening to the patter of rain on the metal roof.

Her keeper allowed her out for breakfast after the big top was raised, and Meg's spirits rose with the number of well-wishes she received from the show people. But the one person she'd hoped to see wasn't in sight. Had Gavin eaten and left already? Dennis was seated with the Cannones, but his father was nowhere to be found.

After breakfast Meg went back to her camper to read the newspaper while Carol caught a ride to the laundromat with the Alexander brothers. Meg would have preferred going along with them to staying alone, but Carol insisted that she rest.

"You never know about head injuries, Meg," Carol said. "Besides, doing laundry is a headache and you already have one."

"Ha. Ha." Meg wrinkled her nose at Carol's impish grin.

"I'll try not to shrink any of your stuff," Carol tossed over her shoulder on her way out the door.

"Thanks."

When Gavin and Dennis stopped by an hour later, Meg was glad she hadn't gone.

"Hi," she said enthusiastically, inviting them in. "Boy, am I glad to see you two guys. I was just getting ready to go out looking for someone to talk to."

"The doctor told you to rest and take it easy for the next couple of days," Gavin pointed out, slipping off the hood of his slicker. "You'd better stay put."

"You sound like Carol." Meg rolled her eyes. "A person could die of boredom following that prescription."

"You could come over and play a game with me," Dennis volunteered. "Or we could watch television together."

"Well, thank you, Dennis. Are you sure you wouldn't rather play with Rico?"

"He has a sore throat and fever, so he can't play." The child's expression drooped with disappointment.

"Oh, that's too bad. I was wondering why I didn't see him with you at breakfast. I'd love to play a game with you." Meg's eyes flew to Gavin's sober face. "That is, if it's all right with your father."

"Sure. It's okay." His tone wasn't very enthusiastic, and Meg got the feeling that perhaps it wasn't.

They walked over to his trailer together, but Gavin didn't go inside.

"I have more work to do. I'll see you later," he said, striding off.

Meg watched him walk away and wondered why he was acting so distant. Last night when he'd held her in his arms and kissed her so tenderly, she'd been sure that he cared for her. But then he'd left abruptly and now he was treating her as if she had the plague. What was going on?

After an hour of playing Pick Up Sticks and several card games, Dennis turned on the television.

"Do you have a television guide?" Meg asked.

"No. We just flip stations to see what's on," Dennis said. "Hey! Do you like baseball?" he asked, tuning in to a major league game. His bright expression told her she'd better.

She smiled. "Yes, I like baseball." After fifteen minutes of watching the game and hearing all about what players were good and what players weren't, Meg felt her eyes growing heavy.

"Dennis, if you don't mind, I'm going to stretch out for a few minutes to rest my eyes."

The boy grinned at her from his cross-legged position on the floor in front of the television. "Sure, that's okay. My dad does that during games sometimes, too."

A few hours later, Meg awoke to the clatter of dishes and voices speaking in hushed tones. She sat up and stretched, realizing that she was still in Gavin's trailer and it was still daylight. The rain had stopped, and the sun was shining brightly around the edges of the closed blinds at the window.

A blue square of fabric fell from her shoulders to the floor, and she bent to pick it up, recognizing the soft item as an old baby blanket. Its satin edge was tattered, as if it had been worn from years of use. Meg smiled. Had Dennis covered her with this? He must have. She couldn't see Gavin covering her with something that obviously belonged to a child.

Tenderness filled her. What a sweetheart Dennis was. Folding the blanket lovingly, Meg laid it at one end of the sofa. She had to thank him.

Gavin and Dennis were in the kitchen when she entered. Gavin was at the stove, stirring a delectable-smelling stew, and Dennis was laying out silverware.

The child looked up. "Hey, Dad, she's awake."

Gavin turned, and Meg smiled at them both.

"I'm sorry I fell asleep. Thank you for covering me with your blanket, Dennis. That was very thoughtful."

The boy shrugged, as if embarrassed, and Meg rescued him by changing the subject.

"Who won the game, anyway?"

"The Cubs beat the Pirates. It was a good game," the child stated, as if she'd really missed something spectacular. "You wanna eat with us? I can set another plate." The boy turned to his father. "She can, can't she, Dad?"

Gavin nodded, and the boy beamed, then opened the cabinet as if it was all decided.

"Thank you for the invitation. Whatever you're cooking smells good." Feeling awkward, Meg studied Gavin, whose dark, wet hair and soapy fresh scent indicated he'd just showered. He was dressed in a clean yellow circus T-shirt and cutoff blue jeans.

He eyed her warily in return. "How are you feeling?" he asked.

"Much better. My headache is gone."

"Good. Did you change your bandage today?"

"Yes, this morning after breakfast." She smiled nervously. Their polite conversation was so stilted. Why were they acting like two strangers? she wondered.

Without Dennis's bright conversation, the meal would have been very uncomfortable. Once Meg got past raving over the food, she had a hard time thinking of what to say to Gavin. And he seemed to be having as much trouble as she. Meg kept catching him staring at her when he thought she wasn't looking.

After dinner, Meg helped clear the dishes and dry them as Gavin washed and Dennis put them away.

"Hey, this is great," Dennis exclaimed. "We got done fast. Can I go out to play?"

"Yes, but don't get muddy," Gavin warned. "We've got a show soon."

Gavin had made coffee, and he and Meg carried their mugs into the living room with them. Dennis ran outside, leaving them to fend for themselves conversation-wise.

After receiving a few short answers to her questions about what had been happening around the circus grounds that day, she asked, "What would you normally be doing if I wasn't here?"

"Relaxing and watching television."

"Oh, well go right ahead. What kind of programs do you like?"

Gavin shrugged as he got up from the couch to turn on the set. "I'm not particular. I usually just watch whatever happens to be on." He tuned in to an old black-and-white movie and smiled. "Is this okay?"

She nodded, and he returned to the opposite end of the couch from where she was seated. She couldn't help remembering how close they'd sat the last time they were here. Did he remember, too?

"I must confess that I do like old movies," he said, losing his wary look for the first time that day. "The Marx Brothers, John Wayne, well, most everything actually. I used to watch movies a lot when I was younger. My mother worked long, late hours, and watching television was about all I had to do."

Meg thought it sounded lonely. "You sound like me, except I read books to fill my spare time. My parents don't even own a television. 'If it doesn't fit in a suitcase, it's too big to lug around the world' is their motto."

Gavin shook his head. "I can't imagine not having a television."

Meg smiled. "I suppose it does seem odd, since we're living in such a video age, but I must confess that I don't watch mine too often. I still read a lot for entertainment."

He shrugged. "I guess it's all what you're used to. You've lived all over the world, so watching a travel show, or a nature show about animals in certain countries might not seem very interesting to you, but seeing them on TV is the only way I'll ever experience them. TV has a lot of great stuff." He tilted his head and frowned. "Don't you watch the news every day?"

She shook her head. "No, I usually just read the newspaper."

"Oh." Gavin looked away to the movie that was on the screen and drank his coffee.

Meg sipped her own coffee and waited, but Gavin had retreated into his shell. She sighed, and finished her coffee.

"Well, thanks for dinner. It was really good," she said, standing up a few minutes later. "I'd better get going. I have to figure out a way to cover up this bandage."

"You're going to be in the show?" His tone held surprise.

"Sure. I feel fine, so there's no reason to miss it. The show must go on, as they say."

He smiled and stood up, taking her coffee mug. "Spoken like a true show person. I thought you'd— Well, never mind."

"I'd what? Wimp out because I got a knock in the noggin?" Seeing the guilty expression on his face, she knew that's exactly what he'd thought. She was delighted to prove him wrong. "Shame on you, Gavin Warner. I'm tougher than I look."

"So I'm learning," he replied. "By the way, I like the new act you and Carol put together. With all that happened yesterday, I forgot to tell you."

She smiled. "Thanks."

"You really are full of surprises," he said, setting their two coffee mugs on the end table before he walked her to the door. "Never in a million years did I dream that you could joke around about your fear of snakes." He stopped at the door, and turned, shoving his hands into the back pockets of his cutoffs. The intense look in his eyes took her breath away.

"I—I just want you to know that I admire you for it," he said quietly.

Meg's heart swelled. "Thank you for telling me," she whispered. "That means a lot." Before she could chicken out, she went up on her toes, took his face between her two hands and kissed him, smack dab on the mouth.

His arms instantly wound around her, which was exactly what she'd hoped for.

Meg arched her body closer to Gavin and inhaled deeply as his hands pulled her more fully against him, crushing her breasts against his chest.

He deepened their kiss, and Meg thought she would burst from the wanting that swelled inside her. He did care for her! Her heart sang with the joy of it.

She could have spent the rest of the afternoon standing within the circle of Gavin's embrace, but parted her lips from his reluctantly. He, as well, seemed unwilling to end their kiss, and feathered a string of light nibbles up her cheek to her temple. He lifted his head when his lips intercepted the square gauze bandage.

"Are you sure you'll be okay doing the show?" His husky voice was tinged with concern.

"Yes." She smiled, touched. "Got any ideas about how I can cover up my bandage?"

He tilted his head and looked at the gauze. "How about fastening a big orange flower in your hair and letting it fall down over your forehead?"

She raised her brows. "Hey, that's a good idea. Thanks."

He smiled. "Glad I could help."

She caressed his cheek with her palm. "You always seem to be helping me. I don't know when I've ever been so well looked after," she said thinking back to all the considerate things he'd done for her. "I don't know what I'm going to do without you when I go back to Rockford," she said huskily, coming as close as possible to telling him how she felt about him without actually saying the words.

He took her hand from his cheek and kissed her palm. "You'll manage just fine without me, I'm sure," he said, backing off. Releasing her hand, he opened the door. "I'll see you later."

Disappointed by his emotional retreat, she removed her slicker from the hook by the door and walked down the wooden steps. After she'd taken several steps, he called after her.

"Meg!"

She stopped and turned. "What?"

"If you see any bicycles on the midway, run!" The grin that split his face was infectious, and she smiled back.

"You bet I will!" she called, waving as she turned toward clown alley, her heart lighter than it had been a minute before.

For the next two days, Meg continued to allow the people around her to pamper her, not because she felt she needed it, but because it seemed to make them feel better. She went back to setting up and taking down the big top on the third day, insisting she was fine. She also wanted to go back to riding, but Gavin wouldn't hear of it until she got her stitches out.

He drove her to a clinic one morning where a doctor removed the sutures, then pronounced her fit enough to return to her regular activities.

"Now will you let me ride again?" she asked Gavin on the way back to the circus grounds.

"Yes, now I'll let you ride again," he echoed, mimicking her exasperated tone.

"You know that I'm probably going to be sore as heck after not riding for a week," she groused.

He glanced at her with his brows raised innocently. "So, use the—"

"Don't say it!" she commanded, raising her hand to stop him. "*Use the liniment!* You've got liniment on the brain, Warner."

He laughed, and she joined him.

Later that afternoon, after Dennis's reading lesson, Meg had her hard hat firmly in place as she walked Misty behind Gavin and Ginger over a grassy hill. She'd enjoyed the scenic mountains, and had been dying to ride ever since they'd entered Pennsylvania.

"Hey, how about picking up the pace a little?" she asked.

Gavin turned around and smiled, his eyes flashing with amusement beneath the brim of his Stetson. "Nag, nag, nag. Be glad you're on that horse, Harper, and don't press your luck!"

Meg wrinkled her nose at him, and he chuckled.

"Hey, look over there." He pointed to a woodsy area, and she halted. "It looks like there's a path through the woods. Let's get out of this sun."

"Okay!"

Following Gavin's lead, she pressed Misty into a canter, thrilled at the wonderful feeling of freedom riding across an open field gave her. Several horse lengths behind Gavin and Ginger, Meg squinted her eyes to read the wood sign posted on the tree next to the path. It was faded and weather-beaten, so she reined in Misty as Gavin entered the woods.

"Private property, no trespassing. Rats! Hey, Gavin!" she shouted. "Come on out of there! Can't you read?"

"What?" He was already too far down the path for her to see him in the dense foliage, but the lack of sound indicated he'd stopped.

"I said, come on out of there!"

Trotting back toward her, he said, "What's up?"

"You'd better start wearing your contacts, buddy. You rode right past a No Trespassing sign. You're either blind, or you can't read," she kidded.

Gavin's eyes widened in shock, and his expression became guarded.

Meg frowned, surprised by his reaction. She'd been joking and had expected him to joke back. Didn't he realize that? Unless...

She watched him carefully as he rode out of the woods.

He glanced back at the sign. "No wonder I missed it. The writing is practically invisible." He shrugged. "I guess we'll have to bypass all that great shade. Man, it seemed ten degrees cooler in there." He turned Ginger, and trotted along the edge of the pasture, riding in the narrow strip of shade cast by the trees.

She frowned after him, amazed by the possible explanation she kept coming up with for his odd behavior. His shocked expression followed so quickly by such forced animation didn't ring true. He was trying to cover up something. Could it possibly be—?

"Are you coming?" he called over his shoulder.

"Yes." She urged Misty into a trot and caught up to Gavin. *Could* it be that he couldn't read? she questioned. The possibility was so astonishing that Meg had trouble keeping her facial expression impassive. She knew she couldn't let Gavin know she suspected he couldn't read until she thought about it a little more. She had to be sure.

Meg was on pins and needles throughout the rest of their ride and that evening she had a hard time concentrating on her performances. By the time she finally fell into bed after taking down the big top, she was exhausted from the questions whirling in her head. By then she'd concluded it was possible that Gavin was illiterate.

She wondered how she could have missed the signs, the inconsistencies in his behavior. Now that she'd had time to think about it, all the clues were so obvious—the lack of newspapers around his trailer, his inability to follow Carol's directions to the hospital, ignoring the No Trespassing sign and the seating sign in the restaurant.

She massaged the scowl from her brow as she lay in the dark. Had he lied to her about wearing contacts that day they'd gone shopping? She'd never noticed them in his eyes. Had he just given that as an excuse because he couldn't read the shipping form he was supposed to fill out for his aunt's gift?

She had to find out for sure. She knew now that she loved him. If he was illiterate, she wanted to help him.

The next morning at breakfast, Meg brought a newspaper to the table and sat across from Gavin.

"Good morning," she said cheerfully.

"Hi. You're here early. Where's Carol?"

"She's still in the shower. I was too hungry to wait, so I came over without her. I've missed seeing you at breakfast. You're usually done by the time I arrive."

"The earlier I start my chores, the earlier I get done," he commented, smiling.

Nervous about what she was about to do, Meg took a deep breath. "There's an article in this morning's paper you might be interested in, since you're such a fan of old movies. It's about someone's collection of black-and-white classics." She held out the newspaper. "Would you like to read it?"

Gavin's gaze lowered to his tray and he swallowed a bite of eggs. "No thanks. I don't have time. I've got a lot of work to do." He gulped his coffee and stood up.

"But you're not done with your breakfast," she protested, feeling guilty for springing the question on him before he'd finished.

"No time." He picked up his tray. "I'll see you later."

Meg wanted to run after him and comfort him as he fled. *Fled.* Meg felt like crying. Gavin *was* trying to hide his illiteracy from her.

The problem was, now that she knew, what was she going to do about it? Gavin had taken such pains to cover his tracks. This was an extremely delicate situation, and she had to handle it properly, or it could be devastating for both of them.

She picked at the eggs on her tray. She no longer had an appetite. For weeks Meg had been wondering why Gavin had been keeping her at a distance. This had to be the reason. He was afraid she'd get too close and learn his secret.

Her heart ached for him. Had he been sitting in on Dennis's lessons hoping to learn to read? If only he'd told her. She could have been teaching him all this time.

She knew that's what she had to do. She had to teach him. There was only a month left before she was supposed to go back to Rockford, but they could make a good start in a month.

But how would she be able to get him to open up about his illiteracy? she wondered. Confronting Gavin about his inability to read was going to be as tricky as walking a tightrope.

That afternoon, after Dennis's reading lesson, Meg dallied at the table. Dennis ran out to play with Rico, which she'd planned on. She didn't want the child to hear whatever was going to happen in the next few minutes. She had no idea how Gavin was going to react, and she didn't want Dennis around to witness Gavin's discomfort when she broached the subject. She had a sneaking suspicion that Dennis knew of his father's illiteracy, since the boy had covered for Gavin on a few occasions that she could recall, but this discussion had to be private.

Gavin was mending again today, but not clothes. He'd brought over a few pieces of tack from the horse tent. The halter he was working on was almost completely stitched. She decided it was time.

Her hands were shaking so badly that she held them in her lap, out of his sight.

"Gavin, do you mind if we have a talk? You don't have to be anywhere right now, do you?"

He looked up, his expression wary. "No. What's up?"

"I want to apologize for upsetting you at breakfast."

"You didn't upset me," he denied, laying aside the mended halter. "I just had a lot of work to do."

"Gavin." She waited until he looked at her. "I know I upset you. I know that you left because you didn't want me to know you couldn't read the article."

His indrawn breath was swift. With lips pressed tightly together, he looked away and stared out the kitchen window.

A heavy silence fell between them, and Meg tensely waited for him to say something. Her heart was breaking for him. She wished she could have softened the blow somehow, but there was only one way she could think of to approach the subject, so she'd been direct.

With his gaze still focused out the window, Gavin's jaw was clenched as he said, "I've been wondering how long it would take you to find out." He stood up abruptly. "Please respect my privacy and don't tell anyone else." Grabbing the leather tack he'd mended, he strode from the room.

Meg jumped up and followed him. "Gavin, wait! Can't we talk about this? I want to help you. Please talk to me!"

Her pleading had no effect. He'd closed her off completely. He didn't even answer. Throwing open the trailer door, his narrowed gaze focused straight ahead as he left.

The pain that ripped through Meg's heart was almost physical. She clutched the doorknob for support and watched Gavin's ramrod straight back retreat from her. He was headed for the horse tent.

Remaining inside his trailer, she closed the door ·and leaned against it. Tears ran freely down her cheeks. She hadn't wanted to hurt him or humiliate him. She'd just wanted to talk to him, to tell him she wanted to help him, but he hadn't listened.

Now what should she do? she asked herself. What could she say to get through to him? How could she make him listen?

Brushing away her tears, Meg found a tissue in the bathroom and blew her nose, then splashed water on her face. The first thing she had to do was get control of her own emotions. She had to be able to think clearly, because she wasn't going to let Gavin run from her again. It was time for her to tear down that wall he'd built between them. He wasn't going to like it, and she was sure he'd try to build it back up again, but she had to try. She loved him too much to give up on him.

Meg gathered her notebook and pencils, dropping them off at her camper, before walking to the horse tent to look for Gavin.

His back was to her as he brushed Ginger's already glistening coat. No one else was around, which wasn't surprising knowing the mood Gavin was in. He'd probably chased everyone away.

"Gavin?"

His body tensed and he paused for a second before continuing the brush strokes down Ginger's left flank. He didn't look at her and he didn't answer.

"I'm not going to go away no matter how much you try to ignore me," she stated stubbornly.

Still he didn't answer.

"Gavin, I want to help you," she said more gently. "Please don't close me off."

"I don't want your help."

"I think you do. I think that's why you've been attending Dennis's lessons for the past six weeks."

"You're the one who said parents should know what their children are doing."

Meg frowned, recalling her words. "That was before I knew you, before I knew that you take an interest in everything Dennis does. You didn't have to sit through every lesson every day to prove that you were interested."

He didn't answer.

"Did you learn anything?" she asked hesitantly.

"Not much. My son is way ahead of me," he muttered, a bitter edge to his tone.

"Why, Gavin?"

"How the hell should I know?" he asked, turning toward her, his eyes snapping with anger. "You're the teacher. You tell me. Maybe I'm stupid."

"Stop it! You know you're not. Otherwise you'd never have been able to fool me into thinking you could read." Taking a deep breath, Meg fought the hurt that tore at her. He was just lashing out in defense. She knew she shouldn't take it personally, but it was hard not to.

As if ashamed of losing his temper, Gavin turned away. "Why don't you just go and leave me alone, Meg?" he said wearily.

"I care about you too much to do that."

He turned, his eyes pleading. "Can't you understand that I don't want your pity?"

"Yes, I understand that very well," Meg walked up to him and, facing him, grasped each of his upper arms. She didn't want him to turn away again. "I respect you far too much to pity you, Gavin. Caring isn't pitying. Did you pity me when I turned to you for help that day I got hysterical about the snake?"

"No, but this is different," he said quietly, his eyes filled with pain.

"I don't see how," she said gently. "When I was young, something happened that made me afraid. You helped me face my fear, and now I've started healing myself. That's all I want to do for you." Unaccustomed to being the aggressor, she squeezed his arms and pleaded, "Talk to me, Gavin. Tell me why you never learned to read. Didn't you go to school when you lived with your mother?"

She could tell her guess was close to the truth by the light that flared in his eyes.

"I went on and off," he said. "Sometimes we weren't in one place long enough to bother registering me for school."

"But you did attend. Didn't any of your teachers question your inability to read?"

He shrugged. "I wasn't very cooperative."

"And no one did anything about it?"

He ran his hand through his hair and stepped back. "The teachers had their hands full just getting me to participate in class. A lot of them didn't really care. They knew I wouldn't be around long." He turned back to the horse and continued brushing the fine chestnut coat as Meg's imagination filled in the rest.

She picked up a comb from the wooden box and walked up to comb the horse's mane. She worked silently alongside Gavin for a few minutes, giving herself time to build up the courage to continue.

Taking a breath, she asked, "What about when you went to live with your aunt and uncle?"

He didn't look at her, and for a moment she thought he wasn't going to answer. She bit her lip, wondering how she could draw him out, but then he replied.

"I went to school."

"And what about your schoolwork? How did you do it?"

"I used to pay other kids to do my homework for me. I earned a lot of money working around my uncle's farm."

"What about tests?"

"I took the math tests, but I used to ditch the other ones unless I knew they were multiple choice. Then I'd just guess."

"And the teachers let you get away with that?" Meg asked, agog.

He shrugged. "I had an excuse for all occasions. Besides—" Gavin frowned "—the teachers knew about my background. They thought I was just a wild kid. I think they felt sorry for my aunt and uncle, so just passed me from grade to grade so Aunt May and Uncle Henry wouldn't be hurt."

Meg pursed her lips. She'd heard about things like this happening, but had never experienced it firsthand before.

She turned and faced Gavin. "I have a month left with the circus. Will you let me teach you?"

He didn't look at her, just kept brushing. "No."

Studying his scowling profile, Meg felt a wave of panic. Now what?

## Chapter Ten

Gavin couldn't look Meg in the eye. He'd known the chances of keeping his illiteracy a secret from her had been slim, and he'd dreaded the time she'd find out. Now that she had, he was as embarrassed as he'd thought he'd be.

Grateful that she hadn't turned from him in disgust, he knew he still couldn't accept her offer to teach him. His pride wouldn't allow it.

"Gavin, why won't you let me teach you?" she asked, placing her hands over his, effectively keeping him from continuing to brush Ginger.

Surprised by her aggressive move and the stubborn tone in her voice, he looked up. Her brilliant blue eyes blazed with determination. What had happened to Meg's shyness? he wondered. The woman facing him now could have fought at Joan of Arc's side.

Warily, Gavin backed away and dropped the brushes into the wooden box. "Meg, leave me a little of my pride, won't you?" he asked, turning away. "Just drop it."

"Pride?" She strode around him and stopped directly in his path so that he was forced to look at her. Her eyes softened with tenderness. "Gavin, I don't want to hurt your pride. I just want to help you. We're friends, aren't we?"

He frowned. "Friends" wasn't adequate for what he felt for Meg, but he nodded. "Yes."

"Then what's wrong with a friend helping out a friend?"

"Meg, this is different." He took the comb from her hand and tossed it into the box with the brushes. "It's bad enough that you found out that I can't read," he said, stepping away, then turning back. He held out his hands. "Can't you understand how embarrassing this is for me?"

"Yes," she replied in a small voice. "I'm not insensitive." Her luminous eyes glistened, and Gavin knew she was close to tears.

"Oh, Meg," he said, striding over and wrapping his arms around her. As she buried her face against his shoulder, he kissed the top of her head. He felt like crying himself. "I know you're not insensitive, honey," he said in a strangled voice. "It's just that this is so hard for me." He swallowed around the lump in his throat. "I tried getting help once," he confessed.

She raised her head. "You did?"

He nodded. "It was when I first found out Lydia was pregnant. Knowing I was going to be a father made me think more responsibly, so I asked Nate for advice and he sent me to a library not far from the circus winter quarters in Florida." He frowned, remembering how nervous he'd been the night he'd walked into that library. "I was embarrassed, but I did it, and I was glad. That night I could hardly wait to get home and surprise Lydia with the news that I was going to take some classes." He smiled wryly. "Well, she was surprised, but not the way I'd expected. She thought that with the baby coming, I'd be better off working a second job at night instead of wasting my time going back to school."

"What did you do?"

He sighed. "I bussed tables at an all-night truck stop diner."

"And you never went back for help after Lydia left?"

"No. The circus is never in one place long enough to get help during the season, and since Lydia left before the circus went to winter quarters, I decided to take Dennis to my aunt and uncle's for the winters from then on. With his mother gone, I wanted him to know he had family who loved him." He turned away, but Meg grabbed his arm and forced him to face her.

"Wait. Why didn't you get help when you were at your aunt and uncle's?"

He paused, uncomfortable with the question. "They don't know I can't read. I didn't want them to find out."

"But why—"

He shrugged away from her. "Because I didn't want them to be disappointed in me!" He lowered his voice. "I couldn't graduate from high school, Meg. I couldn't face them with that after they'd been so wonderful to me." He turned back to her. "This is embarrassing. I'd rather not talk about it anymore."

"Well, you don't have to feel uncomfortable with me, Gavin." She took his hands in hers and looked up. "Please trust me. I promise I won't tell anyone. Just let me teach you to read."

He closed his eyes. Her kindhearted offer was tempting, but he was afraid to accept. What if she couldn't teach him to read? What if there was something wrong with him so that he couldn't learn? How could he stand her disappointment in him?

He shook his head. "Meg, you're leaving in a month—"

"I can teach you a lot in a month."

"Yeah, she can." Dennis's voice behind him took him by surprise.

He released Meg to turn and look at his son. "Dennis, how long have you been there?"

The boy looked up innocently. "Few minutes."

Gavin frowned. "It's not nice to listen to other people's conversations."

"I couldn't help it. Me an' Rico was playin' hide-'n'-seek, an' I was hidin' behind the hay."

"Oh."

Dennis pulled a foil packet of shredded bubble gum from the pocket of his jeans and loaded a small handful of the pink stuff into his mouth. Chewing vigorously, he shoved the foil packet back into his pocket.

"What do you want, Dennis?" Gavin asked when his son made no move to leave.

"I wanna know if you're gonna take readin' lessons from Miss Harper. I think you should, Dad," he added solemnly.

Gavin glanced warily at Meg, who was looking at him expectantly.

"I don't think so, Dennis," he said, turning away from Meg's persuasive gaze.

"How come?"

Feeling as if he was being backed into a corner, Gavin restlessly stepped away, then back. "Dennis, I think I already told you how I feel about this—"

"But Miss Harper knows you can't read," the boy interjected. "It's not a secret anymore."

Gavin shifted uncomfortably. "Dennis, Miss Harper is already giving you reading lessons," he said, grasping at straws. "That's what I traded for giving her riding lessons. I don't want to impose on her—"

"I've got a two-for-one special going this month," Meg interrupted, her expression hopeful. "I'm willing to teach both of you."

Dennis grinned up at Gavin. "Hey, isn't that great, Dad? You're not gonna pass that up, are you?"

Gavin looked back and forth from one to the other. Their expressions were equally expectant. How could he fight them both? He knew he couldn't, and suddenly he didn't even want to. They both obviously cared for him and were trying to get him to do what they thought best. Whatever indignities his pride might suffer would be nothing compared to the guilt he would feel if he let these two down.

"Why do I get the idea you two are ganging up on me?" he asked in resignation.

Meg smiled. "Probably because we are," she said gently.

Dennis just grinned from ear to ear, obviously seeing through his halfhearted attempt at resistance.

"Hey, Dennis!" Rico's call caught the boy's attention. "Why ain't you hidin'?"

Dennis's booted feet were a blur as he ran toward his friend. "I had to talk to my Dad 'bout somethin'," he said. "I'll go hide now."

"Nothin' doin'," Rico protested as the two walked off side by side. "You blew it. It's my turn now."

Shaking his head at the two bickering boys, Gavin turned toward Meg. Her eyes were shining with happiness when they met his.

He sighed, his heart filled with trepidation. "I hope I don't disappoint you, Meg."

"No chance," she assured him.

He smiled, wishing he had her confidence.

She glanced at her watch. "If we skip our ride, we should be able to get a good start on a reading lesson before the first show."

Gavin drew in a deep breath. "I guess I'm as ready now as I'll ever be," he said, his stomach tightening nervously. He took her hand as they walked back to his trailer.

Meg had known Gavin must be bright to function so well in a reading world, but she hadn't guessed how bright. His ability to memorize amazed her. She began to think that that's where his trouble had originally begun when she discovered that instead of analyzing the sounds of the letters in a word, he memorized the word on sight. She quickly broke him of that habit by concentrating on nothing but the alphabet. Once he knew his basic letter sounds and learned to string them together to form a word, Meg couldn't give him new words fast enough. He was like a man who'd discovered an endless supply of water after thirsting in a desert.

Gavin's enthusiasm for learning made their lessons very fulfilling for Meg, and the next few weeks passed all too quickly. The end of the summer was drawing near and she began to worry about what would happen after she left the circus. Could she convince Gavin to leave the circus and settle down somewhere so he could continue his education? she wondered.

Gavin had been more affectionate since she'd begun teaching him, which pleased Meg. It seemed that since he no longer had to hide his secret from her, he felt he could allow his romantic feelings for her to show. Each of the reading sessions ended with a leisurely kiss goodbye at the door of his trailer when Dennis wasn't around, and a few stolen kisses around the darkened circus grounds after the big top came down at night. She still sensed a certain distance in Gavin, though, a holding back, and it worried her.

The circus had wound its way east out of Pennsylvania, then headed south and turned westward. It was now in the mountains of West Virginia.

Riding along a mountain trail behind Gavin one sunny afternoon, Meg inhaled the earthy scent of moist ground and gazed with admiration at the lush beauty of the surrounding woods. Civilization was hidden from sight by dense foliage, the perfect setting for Adam and Eve and romance, she decided.

"You're awfully quiet today," Gavin commented, turning in his saddle to look back at her. His eyes, shaded by the brim of his cream-colored Stetson, were curious.

She smiled. "I've been thinking."

He raised his eyebrows. "About what? The way your eyes are sparkling, it must be something good."

She smiled wider.

His eyes glittered as he caught her mood. "There's a clearing up ahead. Why don't we stop for a few minutes?" he suggested.

"Okay."

They dismounted and tied their horses to a shrub. Meg removed her hard hat, tossing it under a nearby tree as she fluffed her hair with her fingertips.

Gavin took her hand, leading her out of the shade into the center of the sunny clearing.

"God, what a view!" he exclaimed.

Down to their left, the circus tents sat upon a distant grassy knoll. Beyond spread a small town.

"I wish I had my camera," Meg commented, enchanted by the picturesque scene. She pointed to a rocky outcropping a short distance to their left. "Let's sit on that big rock and talk for a while, okay?"

"Just talk?" Gavin asked with a devilish gleam in his eyes.

"For now," Meg commented, slanting him a sideways grin as she strode through the ankle-high grass. She was about to climb up onto the rock when Gavin grabbed her arm.

"Wait a minute. Better let me check this place out for unwanted critters first."

Meg stopped. "Oh. Like those slithery things I can't stand?" she asked, looking around warily.

Gavin climbed up on the flat jutting rock. "I didn't want to say it," he replied, checking around the crevices. He turned back with a smile and extended his hand down to her. "All clear."

Meg reached out and let him help her up. There was plenty of room for them to sit side by side, which they did, dangling their feet over the edge of the six-foot drop-off.

Gavin removed his Stetson, laying it beside him, then wrapped his left arm around Meg's shoulders and pulled her close to his side.

"What a perfect day," he said, looking up at the cloudless blue sky. He glanced down at her. "I can't think of anything I'd rather be doing than sitting here with you."

"Same here," she said quietly, enjoying the way the soft breeze ruffled his hair.

He bent his head and she tilted her mouth up to receive his kiss. Allowing herself to luxuriate in the contentment of the moment, in the sweet rapture of being in Gavin's arms, Meg placed her palm on the yoke of his tan plaid western shirt and felt his heart pound hard beneath it. Knowing that she was the reason it was thumping at such a fast pace was flattering.

Gavin's right hand caressed her stomach, and she caught her breath as the warmth from his hand heated her skin right through her navy circus T-shirt. The tantalizing touch enflamed her senses, and the proximity of his hand to her breasts triggered a heaviness and tingling within her. She'd never before been so aware of her femininity.

Gavin deepened their kiss as his hand moved higher, touching her intimately for the first time, setting off a thermal meltdown that turned her insides warm and liquidy. When his stroking thumb found her sensitive nipple, she covered his hand with her own, knowing the temptation of living for the moment without regard to consequences. But Meg wanted more than a moment. She wanted a lifetime with this man.

Pressing his palm more fully to her breast, she tore her mouth from his, taking comfort from the assertion he must love her to make love to her so exquisitely.

Knowing it would be madness to allow his exploration to go further, until she had his assurance that he cared for her as deeply as she cared for him, Meg gently pried his hand from her breast, lacing the fingers of her left hand through the fingers of his right.

"Gavin, we have to talk," she whispered in a voice so husky she barely recognized it as her own.

He feathered kisses over her brow. "Must we?" he asked between nibbles.

"Yes." Firmly, she pulled away, and he sighed, removing his arm from her shoulders.

Sandwiching her hand between his palms, he looked at her with a tender expression in his warm brown eyes. "Okay. What do we have to talk about?"

Meg swallowed. "I'm supposed to leave in ten days."

Gavin's expression immediately sobered. "I know," he said, frowning, his gaze dropping to their twining fingers.

"Well, I was just wondering what you planned to do about continuing your reading lessons once I'm gone," she asked, studying his profile, hoping he would pick up on her train of thought and declare himself.

His frown deepened. "I don't know yet."

"You're doing so well. Please don't give up," she pleaded.

"I don't want to."

"Gavin." She waited until he looked up, then said, "You need a professional teacher." She looked down as she stroked the tanned skin of his bare forearm with her free right hand. "I just thought you might consider leaving the circus and settling somewhere so you could go back to school."

One corner of his mouth lifted wryly. "It's funny you should say that. I've been thinking about going back to my aunt and uncle's farm in September. I want Dennis to go to first grade in a regular school." He sighed and gazed toward the circus tents in the distance. "It's hard to think about leaving the circus, though. It's been home for a long time. I'm going to miss it."

Looking down, he squeezed her hands and said softly, "I'm going to miss you, too." Checking his watch, he abruptly let go of her and said, "We'd better head back."

The finality in his voice was a death knell for Meg's hopes. He'd miss her, but obviously he could live without her. Otherwise he would have sounded her out about including her in his plans. Wouldn't he?

Too hurt to face him, she scrambled off the rock while he slid his Stetson back on his head. The need to get away shot her full of adrenaline. She covered a distance of several yards before he noticed her flight.

"Meg, what's the rush? Hey, wait up!"

Not pausing to answer or look back, she strode uphill to where the horses were tied.

The thud behind her was followed by a quick curse. "Meg, wait!"

A quick glance over her shoulder indicated Gavin had landed wrong when he'd jumped down from the rock. He favored one foot for a few steps, but didn't look seriously injured. She spared him no more attention.

Leaning down, she scooped up her hard hat and plopped it on her head. Grabbing Misty's reins, she mounted and turned the horse back the way they'd come before Gavin was halfway to his mount.

"Meg! What's wrong?"

Gavin's call didn't affect her. She'd hardened her heart against him. Her spine stiffened with righteous indignation. If Gavin didn't love her, what had all that kissy-touchy stuff been? Merely lust? *Well, to hell with you, Gavin Warner!*

Picking her way down the path, Meg wished she could have spurred Misty into a gallop, but she wasn't crazy. They were headed down a mountain and the path was steep in areas, rocky in others. She wanted to get away from Gavin, but she wasn't willing to kill herself in the process. Her only comfort was knowing she had a good head start and that Gavin would have to use caution in negotiating the path as well.

She didn't hear anything behind her, but once she broke from the woods, she let Misty have her head and crouched low on the galloping mare. Meg's heart soared with the feeling of freedom riding gave her. Gavin might not love her, but she'd always be grateful to him for teaching her to ride.

Unfortunately the distance across the grassy knoll from the woods to the circus grounds wasn't very great, and she had to rein Misty in and walk her to the horse tent.

Tom, Gavin's assistant, was sitting on a bale of hay with Dennis.

"Hi, Miss Harper!" the child called. "Tom's teachin' me to whittle."

Meg smiled, her heart breaking a second time as she glanced at the boy whom she'd grown to love and realized she'd have to say goodbye to him after all. Her eyes began to fill again, and she turned away so he wouldn't see.

"Tom, would you mind doing me a big favor and rub down Misty for me?" she asked, dismounting. "I have something really important I have to do right now."

"Sure, Meg." He jumped up and Meg handed him the reins.

"Thanks, Tom. Good girl, Misty," she said, patting the mare's neck. "Good girl, you did it."

"Did what?" Dennis piped up.

"She got me back here before Ginger and your dad." Meg released Misty as Tom led the horse away.

"You mean you beat Dad in a race?" Dennis asked, wide-eyed.

Meg smiled wryly. "Sort of, but I had a head start."

"Oh." Dennis nodded sagely, as if he knew there had to be a good reason, and Meg fought the temptation to hug the precious boy.

"See you later, guys," Meg called around the lump in her throat. "Thanks again, Tom."

Meg strode to her trailer. Carol was seated outside in a lounge chair sunning herself.

She looked up from a magazine. "Have a good ride?"

"No, I'm afraid not," Meg said quietly, pausing next to the blonde. "Listen, I need to be alone for a while. If anyone wants me, will you do me a favor and tell them I'm not here?"

Her friend's concerned frown helped soothe Meg's raw hurt.

"Does anyone mean *everyone?*" Carol asked with raised eyebrows.

"*Everyone.*"

"Do you want to talk about it, Meg?"

She shook her head and smiled her thanks. "Maybe later. It hurts too much right now."

Carol closed her eyes and waved Meg inside the trailer. "Then I haven't seen you and I don't know when you'll be back. Your privacy is assured."

"Thanks." Meg closed the door behind her and collapsed onto her bed. Burying her face in her pillow, she bit her lip against the pain that tore at her heart.

Gavin rode onto the circus grounds, wondering what he'd done to upset Meg. He thought she'd be glad that he was going back to the farm so Dennis could go to school.

When he'd realized she was running from him, he'd been so dumbfounded, he'd just stared. Unfortunately that had cost him precious time. He probably would have been able to catch up to her if he hadn't twisted his ankle jumping off that rock. Damn bad timing.

As he'd expected, Meg was nowhere in sight when he rode into the horse tent. Tom and Dennis were waiting for him.

"Boy, Dad, you musta really given Miss Harper a big head start," Dennis commented. "She beat you good."

Gavin could tell Dennis was disappointed in his apparent lack of horsemanship, but he wasn't in the mood for long explanations. "She's a fast learner, Dennis," he said, dismounting.

Tom took the reins. "Nate wants to see you right away, Gavin. He said it's real important."

Gavin's eyes narrowed. "Did he say what it was about?" he asked, wondering if it had anything to do with Meg.

"Nope. Just said he wanted to see you soon as you got back an' said I should make sure I told you it was important. I'll take care of Ginger."

"Thanks. Dennis, you'd better go dress for the show while I'm gone."

"Okay, Dad, but look what I did first." He held up a thin stick. "Tom taught me how to whittle."

Seeing how proud Dennis was of his accomplishment, Gavin stooped and examined the stick and the small pile of shavings at Dennis's feet.

"That's great, pal. You just make sure you're careful with that knife. Wouldn't want you losing any fingers."

"I was careful. Tom told me he wouldn't let me borrow his knife if I wasn't."

"Okay." Gavin took the pocketknife from his son's hand and folded it, handing it back to Tom. "Time to get dressed. I'll be along as soon as I talk to Nate."

Gavin knocked at the office trailer.

Nate answered the door, which Gavin thought odd, since the rotund circus owner usually just yelled out his permission to enter.

"Come in, my boy," Nate said, patting Gavin on the back in a fatherly fashion. "Sit down. I have some bad news."

Gavin's heart lurched. Was it about Meg?

"It's about your uncle," Nate said, catching Gavin off guard.

"Uncle Henry?"

Nate nodded solemnly as he plopped into his wooden desk chair. "Got a message from your aunt that he's had a stroke. She wants you to come right away." He handed Gavin a piece of paper. "Here's the phone number of the hospital in case she's not home when you arrive. The doctor's name is Anderson."

Gavin stared at the paper in Nate's outstretched hand, trying to come to grips with what he'd been told. Uncle Henry? In the hospital? *"Never been sick a day in my life,"* he could still hear his uncle brag in his booming voice. *"I'm as healthy as a horse."* And he had been. Uncle Henry was as robust a man as he'd ever met, and Gavin couldn't believe he had had a stroke. Aunt May must be beside herself with worry. He'd have to drive out there right away. Thank God he was only a few hours away from their Kentucky home.

Gavin took the paper with the hospital's phone number. "Thanks, Nate. I... I'll give Tom some instructions first. He's a good kid. You can depend on him." He swallowed hard. "I'll be back as soon as I can."

Nate nodded, his bushy eyebrows drawn together in a concerned frown. "If you need anything, you know where to find me." He stood up and walked around the desk. "I expect you'll want to be on your way. I have to get dressed, so I'll say goodbye now. Show to do, you know." He handed Gavin an envelope. "Here's your pay with a little something extra in case your aunt needs you longer than you counted on."

Gavin stood up. "Thanks, but you—"

Nate waved aside his protest. "Hope all goes well with your uncle. From what you've told me, he's a tough old buzzard. He'll pull through all right."

Gavin shook his outstretched hand and nodded, too choked up to reply. Nate had been his friend as well as his boss for the past twelve years. He was the only person besides Meg and Dennis who knew of his inability to read. He knew he could count on Nate for just about anything.

Gavin strode directly to the horse tent after leaving Nate's office. Several of the cowboys for the Wild West act were already dressed and saddling their horses. Dennis stood beside his pony.

"Hey, Dad, you better hurry up and change."

Gavin shook his head. "I just found out Uncle Henry's sick, Dennis. We have to go see him right away. You're going to have to go change again. We're not going to be in tonight's show after all."

"No?" Dennis's eyes were as big as saucers. He knew missing shows was just not done.

"No. Wait for me in the trailer. I'll be along soon."

Gavin spoke to Tom, letting him know he'd be in charge of the horses while Gavin was gone and giving him a few reminders. Tom had been Gavin's assistant for four years, so he knew he was leaving the horses in capable hands.

After he left the horse tent, Gavin knew he had to make one more stop before leaving the circus. He couldn't leave without talking to Meg.

Clown alley was a hive of colorful activity. Gavin spotted Meg across the tent and dodged several people to get to her.

"Hey, cowboy, haven't you come to the wrong place to get dressed?" Clancy, the head clown, asked.

"I've got to talk to Meg."

"Hey, Big Bertha," Clancy's singsongy voice rang out. "Man to see you."

## *Chapter Eleven*

Meg knew who had come to see her without turning around.

"I'll handle this, Meg," Carol stated, striding toward Gavin. She put out her hand. "Hold it right there, buster. She doesn't want to talk to you."

Meg bent down to tie the laces on her floppy shoes and ignored Gavin as best she could.

"I *have* to talk to her," he said, gesturing with his hands spread wide.

How could he come here now? Meg wondered. He had to know this was the worst possible time to have what could only be an emotional discussion. Concentrating on her performance would be hard enough without talking to him.

"Not now," Carol stated firmly. "We've got a show to do and you've upset her enough for one day."

"But what did I do to upset her?"

Glad she'd asked Carol to run interference for her, Meg headed out of the tent with several other clowns.

"I'd say it was probably what you *didn't* say that upset her," Carol offered.

Overhearing, Meg cringed at her friend's bluntness. She wished Carol hadn't said that.

"What does that mean?" he demanded.

"Figure it out. But for now, leave her alone, Gavin. She has a show to do and so do I. This will have to wait for another time. *Goodbye.*"

As they lined up for the Spectacle Parade, Meg squeezed her friend's hand. "Thanks."

"No problem. That's what friends are for. I wish you'd followed your own advice, though. Falling for a showman isn't the smartest thing you've ever done, Meggie," Carol blustered. Giving Meg an affectionate hug, Carol said, "Now, chin up! Paste on that big smile of yours and remember you're a professional."

"I know," Meg said as she dunked a plastic wand in her oversize bottle of suds. "The show must go on."

So, she did.

Meg got through both shows that night, and though she knew neither of her performances were sparkling, she hadn't missed any cues. She'd purposely avoided looking for Gavin during the shows and was relieved that she'd never accidentally caught a glimpse of him.

Worried that he might try to talk to her between shows, Meg was glad that he didn't show up. He was obviously taking Carol's advice and respecting her privacy for now. Not sure how long her reprieve would last, Meg tried to figure out what to tell him once he was tired of biding his time.

Taking down the big top that night, Meg was surprised there was no sign of Gavin anywhere. The huge folded canvas was being rolled onto the spool truck before she found out why.

Tom, Gavin's assistant, called to her as she and Carol were walking to their camper. "Meg, wait up!" His low voice carried in the eerie silence of the circus that had been all but put to bed.

Meg turned, and her heart lurched at Tom's sober expression. Fearing that either Gavin or Dennis had had an accident, she quickly asked, "Is something wrong?"

Tom stopped and jammed his hands into the rear pockets of his jeans. "Yeah. Gavin's uncle had a stroke. He and Dennis had to leave. Gavin asked me to tell you."

Meg's stomach tightened into a knot. "When did they leave?"

"During the first show. Nate gave him the message as soon as he got back from his ride with you."

"Oh." Meg swallowed hard, guilt pressing down on her as she realized that that had probably been the reason for his wanting to talk to her. How awful that she hadn't allowed him to explain!

"Is his uncle going to be all right?" she asked, concern welling inside her. She knew Gavin cared for his uncle and must be very worried.

Tom shrugged. "Don't rightly know."

"Did Gavin say anything else?" Carol asked.

"Nope. That was it."

Knowing what Carol was driving at, Meg forestalled her friend. "Thanks, Tom."

He nodded his head at both of them and said, "Good night."

Speaking in hushed tones so she wouldn't wake anyone who was already in bed, Meg grasped her friend's arm. "Carol, I feel terrible! I didn't even give Gavin the chance to tell me himself. I've been so unfair to him."

"Hold it, Meg. Before you start with the guilt, remember that I was the one who told him to buzz off."

"But only because I asked you to."

They climbed into their camper and changed clothes in silence. Lying in bed, unable to sleep, Meg wished she could turn back the clock and change the way she'd handled things.

Carol whispered to her in the darkness. "You know, neither of us is a mind reader, Meg. There's no way we could have known that Gavin wasn't there to talk about precisely what we thought. We really shouldn't feel guilty."

"*You* shouldn't," Meg agreed, "but I can't help it. I should have known Gavin wouldn't have tried to talk to me right before a show without a darned good reason."

*I should have known,* Meg thought to herself. But now, because of her hurt pride, she hadn't had a chance to say goodbye to Gavin or offer him any comfort. She hadn't said goodbye to Dennis, either.

Her heart lurched. What if they didn't return to the circus before it was time for her to leave? In ten days she'd be returning to her quiet little house in Rockford, Illinois. The prospect wasn't as attractive now as it had been earlier in the summer. There would be no one there but her. She'd be returning to her normal, but lonely, loveless life, and might never get to see Gavin or Dennis again! She choked back tears.

How odd that for the past several years she'd thought of her house as *home* when she realized now that she didn't have a place to call home. If only wishing could make it so...

Gavin arrived at his aunt and uncle's farm after nightfall. The house and yard lights were on, so he assumed his aunt was home from the hospital. Parking his trailer next to the barn, he gently shook Dennis, who'd fallen asleep next to him on the bench seat of the pickup.

"Wake up, pal. We're here."

Dennis sat up, clutching his ragged blue baby blanket as he rubbed his eyes.

Knowing how unhappy his son was at having to leave the circus without saying goodbye to either Rico or Meg, Gavin hadn't said anything to Dennis about carrying the blanket along in the pickup, even though it normally stayed under his pillow in the trailer. He still remembered the jolt it had given him to see the blanket spread over Meg's shoulders the day she'd fallen asleep on his couch. If Dennis received comfort from hugging his security blanket, Gavin was glad.

He empathized with his son's misery. Leaving without being able to speak to Meg had been torture. Knowing that Tom would inform her of the reason he'd had to leave wasn't the least bit satisfactory. He'd wanted to explain himself and straighten out their misunderstanding.

Carol's words had been haunting him ever since he'd left the circus grounds. Meg was upset because of what he *hadn't* said.

He'd *said* he'd miss her. Could she have wanted to hear that saying goodbye to her was going to be the hardest thing he'd ever done in his life? Or did she want more? Did she want a declaration of love? He hardly dared hope.

Frustration gnawed at him and he ran his hand restlessly through his hair. If only he'd had the time to find out.

Gavin was relieved to hear that his Uncle Henry's condition had stabilized, though his left side had been left partially paralyzed. His uncle's prognosis was good, and after a week he was released from the hospital and placed in a nursing home.

Gavin sympathized when the old codger grumbled about not being allowed to go home. It was hard to be stuck in one place when you longed to be in another. Knowing that Meg was due to leave the circus in a few days, Gavin, too, was chomping at the bit, but he knew he couldn't leave until he had his uncle settled.

"You need therapy, Henry," his Aunt May argued as she fluffed a pillow and carefully put it behind his uncle's gray-haired head after he'd been placed in his private room at the nursing home. "You'll be able to get it here."

"I need to see to my horses. Portia's due to foal—"

"Portia's fine," Gavin soothed from the foot of the bed. "The vet was out yesterday. You need to concentrate on getting well. Cole's a good stablehand. The two of us can handle the horses."

His uncle sighed and stared down at his left arm, which lay limply at his side. "I feel so dang useless," he drawled, then looked up. "I'm sorry, Gavin. This is unfair to you. You got your own life to lead, and here you are havin' to look after me an' the farm."

"Hey, cut it out, Uncle Henry."

His uncle shook his head, his expression downcast. "No, it isn't fair to you. You're a good boy for comin' to my rescue, Gavin, but I'm gettin' old. Can't do all the things I used to do anymore. That's why I hired on Cole." He reached for his wife's hand with his right one and looked up into her eyes. "What do you think, May? Should we sell off the place?"

"Henry, that's our home," she scolded. "We can't sell it. You know you'd never be happy anyplace else, and neither would I." She smoothed a gray strand of his thinning hair back from his forehead. "You're just not feeling good right now, or you wouldn't even say such a thing. When you get better you'll think differently. In the meantime Gavin has said he'll stay on to help—"

"But it's not fair to the boy, May. How can we ask him to stay knowing how he hates it?"

"Whoever said I hated it?" Gavin demanded, capturing his aunt and uncle's attention.

"Perhaps Uncle used too harsh a term," his aunt began, looking his way, "but we know you'd rather be traveling with the circus. You've got your mother's wanderlust in your blood—"

"No, I don't," he denied. "I *love* the farm, and I'm willing to stay for as long as you need me or want me." Gavin knew his uncle would wither and die if he sold his farm. He couldn't allow Uncle Henry's temporary depression to cloud his thinking.

"You don't have to say that, boy." His uncle smiled. "It does my heart good to know you're willing to stay on because you care for us, but I can't allow you to make that sacrifice."

"It's no sacrifice," he denied. "In fact, I've been thinking about coming back here to live permanently."

"But you ran away." His aunt's expression grew puzzled. "You told us you wanted to see the world."

Unable to look his aunt and uncle in the eyes, he walked to the window, knowing this was as far as he could run. The time for lies and excuses had come to an end. It was time to stand and tell the truth once and for all.

Gavin took a deep breath, relieved that he'd finally decided to make a clean breast of his illiteracy. He'd tell no more lies; there would be no more hiding, no more shame. He'd turn his life around for the better, or at least try. With the help of the people he loved, he just might succeed.

Remembering how Meg had held her head high the day she'd left his trailer after sharing the burden of her snake phobia with him, he lifted his head and calmly turned and faced his aunt and uncle.

"Aunt May, please take a seat. I have something to tell you both."

The circus wound out of West Virginia into Kentucky, and Meg wondered where within the state Gavin's aunt and uncle's farm was located. She'd never thought to ask, not that knowing would do her any good. Thoughts of them sitting around a cozy kitchen table eating soup from the tureen Gavin had sent his aunt made her happy.

The circus was located just outside of Lexington two nights before Meg and Carol were due to leave. Meg lingered at the back door at the end of the first show and scanned the audience as it left the big top. She was haunted by the sensation that Gavin and Dennis were near, and could have sworn she'd heard Dennis's high-pitched laughter during her camping act with Carol.

As the big top emptied without her spotting them, she shrugged, attributing her imaginings to wishful thinking. After all, one child's laugh was much like another's, she told herself, and the tent had been full of children. Still, the strange sensation persisted as she walked back to clown alley. Meg scoffed at herself. Maybe Rosa Cannone's talk of omens was getting to her.

Just yesterday Meg had overheard Rosa telling Gabriella Giovani, a tightrope walker, that she'd heard one of the roustabouts whistling as he'd rolled a bale of hay into the horse tent on the day Gavin had received the news of his

uncle's illness. Stuff and nonsense to Meg's way of thinking, but Gabriella had raised her eyebrows and nodded as if
she believed every word.

Meg entered clown alley and sat in her regular seat next
to Carol. She helped the rest of the clowns blow up long,
skinny balloons and twist them into animal shapes. A group
of children from a nearby orphanage were expected at the
next show. The clowns would be making more balloon figures for the children during the show, but Nate wanted to
make sure there were enough to go around. He didn't want
them leaving without a souvenir.

As they worked, Clancy, the head clown, asked if they
might be back with the show next summer.

"I doubt it," Carol said, smiling at Meg. "I was lucky I
got Meg to agree to this summer. She hates traveling, you
know, and once she gets back to her house, I'm sure I won't
be able to budge her."

"Well, come by yourself then," Clancy encouraged.

"Thanks for the offer, but I don't think so. Pansy and Big
Bertha are partners. It just wouldn't be the same."

Clancy shrugged and walked away, and Carol leaned over
to Meg and whispered, "I didn't want to tell him my real
reason."

"What is your real reason?" Meg asked quietly.

Carol waved her closer and whispered directly into her
ear. "I couldn't stand to spend another summer in the
company of Kurt and Ivan Alexander. They may be hunks,
but they're so obnoxious!"

Meg laughed, her first genuine laugh since the day Gavin
had left, and she leaned back in her chair to stretch with the
joy of it. With her arms extended over her head, her hands
struck someone behind her.

"Excuse me," she said automatically, turning in her chair
to see whom she'd hit. The prickling sensation on the back
of her neck warned her too late. Gavin stood smiling down
at her, his unexpected presence knocking the wind right out
of her.

"I always seem to be sneaking up and taking you by surprise. Sorry." His big grin said he wasn't sorry at all, and Meg just stared in dumb wonder, drinking in the wonderful sight of him dressed in gray slacks and a navy sports shirt. She'd never seen him so dressed up.

"Meg, Carol, I'd like you to meet my aunt. Aunt May, this is Meg Harper, better known as Big Bertha, and her friend Carol Callahan, known as Pansy."

Meg staggered to her feet and glanced at the tall, thin woman in a rose-colored skirt and blouse standing beside Gavin.

"I'm pleased to meet you, Meg," she said, extending her hand. "I've heard a lot about you."

Shocked, Meg automatically shook hands. "I—I've heard about you, too. How— How is your husband?"

"He's doing very well. He's in a nursing home for therapy right now, but the doctor thinks he has a good chance of recovering much of the movement he lost in his left side."

"Oh, that's good news. I'm happy for you," Meg answered, unable to look at Gavin, even though she was extremely aware of his presence beside her.

"Gavin and Dennis decided I needed a night out after all the worry of the past week, so they brought me to see the circus and meet all of their friends." Gavin's aunt squinted as she apparently tried to pick out Meg's real features beneath the makeup, and Meg smiled.

"I'm sorry I can't take my makeup off, I have another show to do tonight."

"Actually, you don't," Gavin contradicted, then smiled when she glanced at him with wide eyes. "Ah, I see I've finally captured your attention."

"What do you mean?" Meg asked.

"I mean I've asked Nate if I can steal you away for one night, and he said it was okay with him if it's okay with Carol." Gavin turned to Carol. "What do you say, Pansy? Do you mind if Big Bertha skips out on you for one show?"

"Not if it's for a good reason," Carol answered, studying Gavin.

"It is."

Carol looked at him, then gave her grudging permission. "It had better be."

"Great. Thanks." He turned to Meg. "How soon can you be changed?"

Meg frowned. Though she was delighted at the prospect of spending time with Gavin, she wasn't pleased by his high-handedness.

"Perhaps you should ask Meg's permission, dear," his aunt suggested. "After all, she may not want to miss the show."

Meg smiled at Gavin's aunt, immediately liking her. The woman was very perceptive.

"Meg?" Gavin asked. "You will come with us, won't you?"

"Where?" she asked, exasperated by the quandary in which she found herself. Her eagerness to go with Gavin warred with her sense of responsibility to Carol and the show.

"I want to take you to see the farm."

The farm of cozy kitchen fame? Meg could have resisted anyplace, but that. She turned to Carol. "If you're sure you don't mind."

"I don't." Carol's eyes twinkled and Meg could clearly read the message there. Her friend was telling her to go for it.

Meg smiled gratefully, then turned to Gavin. "All right."

"Great. We'll pick you up at your camper later. I'm going to take Aunt May over to the Cannone trailer. Dennis is there already. He couldn't wait to see Rico." Gavin leaned close and quietly added, "He's anxious to see you, too." His velvety tone strummed along her nerves with warm intimacy.

Meg showered in her camper before she changed clothes. With Gavin and his aunt all dressed up, she wasn't about to appear all sweaty and gritty when they came for her. She let her hair air dry as she applied a light amount of makeup, then dressed in the only nice clothes she'd brought along.

Her forest-green blouse looked dressy but casual with her khaki skirt and wide brown belt. Low-heeled brown pumps completed the outfit, and Meg paced in the small confines of the camper as she waited for them to come for her.

She knew she was leaving herself wide open for more heartache, but her hopes were high that Gavin had a good reason for taking her to see the farm. She decided that if he asked her why she'd been upset, she wouldn't evade his question. If she didn't take the initiative, her dreams might never have a chance of coming true.

A knock at the door was followed by Gavin's voice. "Meg, are you ready?"

She opened the door and stepped down, cautiously eyeing Gavin. His eyebrows shot up and his smile told her he approved of her outfit.

"Wow!" Dennis exclaimed. "You sure look pretty, Miss Harper."

Meg smiled, and gave the boy a quick hug. "Thank you. You look pretty spiffy yourself."

Dennis shrugged, but Meg could tell he was pleased by her compliment, though he wouldn't admit it. Wearing dress slacks and a good shirt went against a six-year-old boy's code of acceptable dress.

May Warner smiled at her. "I feel like I'm meeting you all over again. You're very pretty, Meg."

"Thank you."

"It seems a shame to cover up that beautiful face with all that clown makeup," May continued.

"Amen," Gavin concurred, but Meg made no reply.

"The farm's about a half-hour's drive from here," he announced, taking each woman by the hand as Dennis skipped along beside them.

"That close?" Meg asked, wishing it were farther away so she'd have that much more time with them.

"Yes, my husband and I are both from the Lexington area," May Warner commented. "Henry's grandparents used to own our farm, so it's been in the family for a long time."

"Do you have any children?"

"No, Henry and I were never blessed with our own, but we've come to think of Gavin as the son we never had, and Dennis the grandson."

Gavin and his aunt exchanged a loving smile, and Meg was touched by their affection for each other.

Gavin led them to a late-model silver Cadillac. "We brought my aunt's car," he explained.

"Oh. I wondered how we were all going to fit in the pickup."

Gavin opened the passenger door, and May told Meg to sit up in front with Gavin. She'd sit in back with Dennis.

Meg smiled at May Warner's attempt at playing matchmaker and wondered what Gavin thought. His expression told her nothing.

The ride to the farm passed pleasantly enough with most of the conversation coming from Aunt May and Dennis. Gavin hardly said a word, which Meg found curious. She answered his aunt's occasional questions, and volunteered a few of her own, but her mind was on the man seated next to her.

When Gavin stopped the car in front of the large white farmhouse, Aunt May said she was going to go in and prepare a light supper for them. Meg offered to help, but the older woman declined her offer, saying Dennis was help enough.

"You go take a walk with Gavin. I'm sure he wants to show you around."

Meg followed as Gavin took her hand and led her across the yard to the stables. Her stomach fluttered nervously as she wondered when he would broach the subject of her running from him that day in the woods.

"Here's my uncle's pride and joy," Gavin said, gesturing down the long row of stalls. "He's been raising and training horses for over forty years."

Now that they were alone together, Meg became tonguetied. She didn't say much in reply to Gavin's comments about each of the horses, just nodded her head and felt the tension inside her wind tighter and tighter.

His enthusiasm for the horses finally penetrated her preoccupation when they reached the stall of a chestnut mare.

"This is Portia. She's due to foal in a couple of weeks." Gavin rubbed the chestnut muzzle that poked out curiously over the stable door.

"She looks just like Ginger," Meg said, stepping closer to allow the horse to sniff her hand.

"She should. Portia's Ginger's mama." He patted the horse, then turned and pointed through a doorway at the end of the building. "Tack room."

Meg glanced in and nodded.

"Lost your voice again?" he asked.

She shrugged. "I guess my mind's just not on horses right now." Walking to the paddock, she leaned her forearms on the top rung of the wooden fence and gazed at the orange sunset.

Gavin stopped beside her. "God, you're beautiful. The sun is highlighting your hair with streaks of gold."

Meg turned to him. He was melting her heart with his words, but she needed to see what was in his eyes. For a heart-stopping moment she reveled in the admiring warmth she found there. Then Gavin glanced at the farmhouse.

"Let's go for a walk," he suggested, taking her hand and pulling her across the yard. "We have a lot to discuss, Meg, and I prefer to do it privately." He led her through a gate and across a field, then through another gate. He stopped before they reached the narrow strip of woods that separated his uncle's farm from the next one over. A creek gurgled a short distance away.

Pointing to the short logs arranged in a circle around a small pile of rocks, Gavin said, "Have a seat."

"What is this place?" Meg asked.

Gavin smiled. "Uncle Henry's getaway. We used to come out here for picnics every summer when I lived here. Uncle Henry likes cooking out over a camp fire, but he never wanted to be too far away from his stable, so he set up this place. Sometimes Dennis and I come here in the winter, too. We ice-skate on the creek, and I build a small fire to warm us up."

Meg sat down on a thick log, momentarily distracted from her thoughts by the ambience of the setting. It would have been quite romantic if there had been a small camp fire crackling in front of them.

Gavin sat on a smaller log next to her. "So what gives, Meg?"

She shook her head. "What do you mean?"

"I *mean*, why did you run away from me?"

## Chapter Twelve

Meg had rehearsed this moment in her mind a dozen times over the past week, but now that Gavin had actually brought up the subject, she found that all her carefully thought out answers escaped her. Staring at the ground in front of her, she rolled a stone with the toe of her brown pumps as she frantically sought the words to form a reply.

*Gosh darn it!* she thought. She was twenty-eight years old and a modern-thinking woman. Why couldn't she tell him that she loved him? Obviously there was some old-fashioned glitch in her personality that insisted the man should do the pursuing.

"Uh-oh. You've gone shy on me again, Meg. I thought we'd gotten past all that." His affectionate teasing was meant to cajole, of course, but it didn't help.

She frowned. "I'm no good at this."

"At what?" he prompted.

"At man-woman stuff." She cringed at her words. Now that was really an intelligent answer, she thought sarcastically.

"Oh, I don't know. You're pretty good at the man-woman stuff *I've* tried with you." His suggestive tone was colored with amusement and Meg's cheeks flamed.

This was not going as she'd planned.

"All right, honey," he said tenderly. "I'll help." He wrapped his left arm around her shoulders. "Perhaps we should start with Carol's suggestion that it wasn't what I'd said, but what I *hadn't* said that upset you."

Meg tensed, and Gavin said "Ahh" very softly.

Part of her rehearsed speech suddenly flashed in her mind, and she glanced up. "Oh. I just thought of something. I meant to apologize first thing—" She paused, collecting herself, then spoke more slowly. "I'm sorry I refused to talk to you the day you left. It was very unfair to you, and I felt badly about it afterward."

He nodded. "This week has been pretty hellish at times. Not knowing what was wrong between us drove me a little crazy, and I hated not being able to say goodbye to you."

"Me, too," she answered, her heart suddenly filled with trepidation. What if he still meant to say goodbye to her?

"Will you tell me why you wouldn't talk to me, Meg?" Gavin's expression was serious.

"I was hurt," she admitted, staring back down at the stone. She nudged it with her toe.

"Why?" He lifted her chin with his fingertips and forced her to face him.

"Because," she whispered, her mouth going as dry as cotton as she gazed up. "You said you'd miss me. You were ready to say goodbye and I wasn't."

His eyes flared. "I didn't think I had a choice—*then*," he stressed. The edges of his mouth turned up in a wry smile. "A lot can happen in a week. I never dreamed how much."

With bated breath, Meg waited for him to elaborate. The setting sun bathed his features in a golden glow, but the light in his eyes came from inside.

"My life turned upside down, Meg, but it righted itself back again. And you know what?"

"What?" she whispered, her eyes riveted to his, watching every nuance of expression.

"It's a lot better now." He paused, but still she waited, knowing he had more to say, and a tiny spark of hope began to grow in her heart.

He raised her palm to his lips and kissed it lightly, then smiled. "I had a long talk with my aunt and uncle, Meg. I told them."

She drew in a swift breath. There was no need to ask about what. "Oh, Gavin, I'm so glad!"

He rubbed her hand between his palms. "So am I. They took it really well." He looked up. "I also told them I want to come back to the farm permanently, and we discussed all my options. They want me to take over the running of the farm, Meg." The pride in his eyes caught at her heart.

"They're going to handle the paperwork until I can manage it," he explained. "I'm going to go back to school at night."

"I'm so happy for you!" she whispered, overcome with joy.

He nodded, his smile dazzling with determination. "Uncle Henry said I may as well learn to run the farm now, since it will be mine someday. They're such wonderful people, Meg."

She nodded. "I like your aunt."

"I think you're going to like my uncle, too." He raised his eyebrows significantly, and Meg knew his statement was more than idle conversation.

"Am I going to get to meet him?"

"You're going to get to do more than meet him," he said, looking into her eyes. "That is, if you want to."

Meg's heart lurched. What was he saying? Was it possible that he—?

Gavin's lips curved upward in a tender smile and he nodded at her questioning gaze. "Do you think you could like living around here?"

"I could like living *anywhere* as long as you were there,"
she declared, smiling expansively. "Even if it was in a traveling circus."

He hugged her and she placed her hands on his chest.

"You know, I thought about that after you left," she
said, frowning as she gazed into his eyes. "I was never sure
exactly *why* I disliked traveling, but I finally figured it out.
It wasn't the *fact* of traveling I minded. It was that I'd never
felt anyone really cared for me." She held up her hand to
stop his questions. "Oh, sure, my parents cared, but they
were too involved in their careers to pay me much attention."

Gavin's eyes narrowed. "What about Mrs. Farnham?"

"We were never that close *emotionally*," she said. "I
guess I felt like I was just a job to her. The first time I really
felt that someone cared about me was when I settled in
Rockford." She looked into his eyes. "But that was nothing compared to the way you made me feel. No one has ever
cared for me so well."

"Oh, Meg." Gavin lowered his head and she lifted her
mouth to his. His urgency seemed to match her own. After
a minute, he pulled back and cradled her jaw in his palm.

"I'll continue to care for you for the rest of your life if
you'll let me," he vowed. "I love you, Meg Harper. Please
say you'll marry me."

"Yes, yes," she whispered happily, raising her face for
another kiss.

Later, as darkness fell, they strolled hand in hand back to
the farmhouse.

"Aunt May is probably dying of curiosity right about
now," Gavin confided.

"She must be wondering what we've been doing all this
time."

Gavin's sideways smile was the most devastatingly sexy
grin Meg had ever seen.

"Oh, I think she has a pretty good idea of what we've
been doing," he suggested, making Meg blush with plea-

sure. "She'll just want to know all the details of how I popped the question."

"She knew you were going to ask me to marry you?" Meg asked in surprise.

He nodded. "Do you mind?"

"No." She slipped her arm around his waist and tilted her face up to his for a quick kiss. "Does Dennis know?"

"Not about us, but I think he'll go for the idea." Gavin smiled. "He's excited about going to school and getting to ride the bus. Aunt May has been filling him in on how his life is going to change, and he can hardly wait."

"What about his friendship with Rico?"

Gavin shrugged. "That he'll miss, but I expect he'll make new friends. He's already got a new hero. You should see the way he follows Cole around. Everything is 'Cole this' and 'Cole that'."

Meg smiled. "Who was his old hero?"

"*Me*, of course." He feigned insult, and she laughed.

"Don't feel bad, you're still my hero."

He pulled her close. "And it better stay that way," he growled playfully, but Meg detected an underlying note of seriousness, reminding her that he'd been hurt by Lydia.

"Hey, I'm a one-hero gal," she assured him.

The yard around the farmhouse was well lit as they approached, and Gavin nodded toward the two-story dwelling.

"I hope you like the house. Aunt May and Uncle Henry's room is on the first floor, so we can have the whole upstairs to ourselves. It's big enough for all of us, but if you'd prefer a place of our own, we don't have to live here."

Meg smiled, thrilled with the thought of being part of a family. "Why don't we live here after we're married and see how it goes? We have lots of time to make up our minds about that."

Gavin pulled her up the steps and into the shadows on the side porch. "How soon can we get married?" he asked, taking her in his arms.

"As soon as I go back to Rockford, resign from my job and make arrangements to sell my house. Is that soon enough?"

"Tomorrow wouldn't be soon enough for me, but I guess that will have to do." He smothered her lips in a kiss that told of his burning need and left her weak with desire.

Hearing voices inside the house, they slowly parted.

"*Soon*, Meg," he demanded huskily, and she nodded, trembling with anticipation.

He slanted one corner of his mouth wryly as he released her. "We'd better go in. We're late for supper."

Gavin opened the side door, and they stepped into a big, old-fashioned country kitchen, warmly cheerful in yellow and bright blue.

Meg's mouth formed an *O* and she gasped with pleasure. The kitchen was as cozy and inviting as she'd imagined.

Aunt May and Dennis were seated at the round oak table.

"Come on in, you two." May Warner gestured for them to sit down. "Dennis and I were hungry, so we started without you."

In the middle of the table sat the soup tureen Gavin had sent his aunt.

Meg knew she was home.

\*     \*     \*     \*     \*

Bestselling author **NORA ROBERTS** captures all the romance, adventure, passion and excitement of Silhouette in a special miniseries.

# THE CALHOUN WOMEN

Four charming, beautiful and fiercely independent sisters set out on a search for a missing family heirloom—an emerald necklace—and each finds something even more precious . . . passionate romance.

Look for THE CALHOUN WOMEN miniseries starting in June.

**COURTING CATHERINE**
in Silhouette Romance #801 (June/$2.50)

**A MAN FOR AMANDA**
in Silhouette Desire #649 (July/$2.75)

**FOR THE LOVE OF LILAH**
in Silhouette Special Edition #685 (August/$3.25)

**SUZANNA'S SURRENDER**
in Silhouette Intimate Moments #397 (September/$3.25)

---

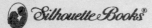
*Silhouette Books* ®

# SILHOUETTE·INTIMATE·MOMENTS®

## IT'S TIME TO MEET
## THE MARSHALLS!

In 1986, bestselling author Kristin James wrote A VERY SPECIAL FAVOR for the Silhouette Intimate Moments line. Hero Adam Marshall quickly became a reader favorite, and ever since then, readers have been asking for the stories of his two brothers, Tag and James. At last your prayers have been answered!

In June, look for Tag's story, SALT OF THE EARTH (IM #385). Then skip a month and look for THE LETTER OF THE LAW (IM #393—August), starring James Marshall. And, as our very special favor to you, we'll be reprinting A VERY SPECIAL FAVOR this September. Look for it in special displays wherever you buy books.

MARSH-1

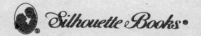

# *Silhouette Special Edition*

proudly hails

## WOMEN OF GLORY

## from Lindsay McKenna

Soar with Dana Coulter, Molly Rutledge and Maggie Donovan—Lindsay McKenna's WOMEN OF GLORY. On land, sea or air, these three Annapolis grads challenge danger head-on, risking life and limb for the glory of their country—and for the men they love!

**May: NO QUARTER GIVEN (SE #667)** Dana Coulter is on the brink of achieving her lifelong dream of flying—and of meeting the man who would love to take her to new heights!

**June: THE GAUNTLET (SE #673)** Molly Rutledge is determined to excel on her own merit, but Captain Cameron Sinclair is equally determined to take gentle Molly under his wing....

**July: UNDER FIRE (SE #679)** Indomitable Maggie never thought her career—or her heart—would come under fire. But all that changes when she teams up with Lieutenant Wes Bishop!

# Take 4 bestselling love stories FREE

## Plus get a FREE surprise gift!

## Special Limited-time Offer

Mail to
**Silhouette Reader Service™**
3010 Walden Avenue
P.O. Box 1867
Buffalo, N.Y. 14269-1867

**YES!** Please send me 4 free Silhouette Romance™ novels and my free surprise gift. Then send me 6 brand-new novels every month, which I will receive months before they appear in bookstores. Bill me at the low price of $2.25 each—a savings of 25¢ apiece off cover prices. There are no shipping, handling or other hidden costs. I understand that accepting the books and gift places me under no obligation ever to buy any books. I can always return a shipment and cancel at any time. Even if I never buy another book from Silhouette, the 4 free books and the surprise gift are mine to keep forever.

215 BPA AC7N

| Name | (PLEASE PRINT) | |
|------|----------------|---|
| Address | | Apt. No. |
| City | State | Zip |

This offer is limited to one order per household and not valid to present Silhouette Romance™ subscribers. Terms and prices are subject to change. Sales tax applicable in N.Y.

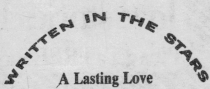
WRITTEN IN THE STARS

## A Lasting Love

The passionate Cancer man is destined for love this July in Val Whisenand's FOR ETERNITY, the latest in our compelling WRITTEN IN THE STARS series.

Sexy Adam Gaines couldn't explain the eerie sense of familiarity that arose each time his eyes met Kate Faraday's. But Mexico's steamy jungles were giving the star-crossed lovers another chance to make their love last for all eternity....

FOR ETERNITY by Val Whisenand is coming this July from Silhouette Romance. It's WRITTEN IN THE STARS!

---

*Silhouette Romance* ®